The
Ocean Forest

I hope you enjoy my story!

W9-AQI-579

The
Ocean Forest

by

Troy D. Nooe

INGALLS PUBLISHING GROUP, INC
PO Box 2500
Banner Elk, NC 28604
www.ingallspublishinggroup.com

copyright © 2011 Troy D. Nooe
Text design by Ann Thompson Nemcosky
Cover painting by JoeBurleson/burlesongraphics@charter.net
Cover design by Luci Mott

This book is a work of fiction. All characters, places and incidents are either the product of the author's imagination or are used fictitiously, and any resemblance to persons living or dead, business establishments, events or locales is entirely coincidental.

Without limiting the rights reserved under copyright above, no part of this publication may be reproduced, stored or entered into a retrieval system or transmitted, in any form or by any means (electronic, mechanical, photocopying, recording or otherwise), without the prior written permission of both the copyright owner and the above publisher of this book. Exception to this prohibition is permitted for limited quotations included within a published review of the book.

The scanning, uploading and distribution of this book via the internet or via any other means without the permission of the publisher is illegal and punishable by law. Please purchase only authorized editions and do not participate in or encourage piracy of copyrighted materials. Your support of author rights is appreciated.

Library of Congress – Cataloging-in-Publication Data
Nooe, Troy D.
The ocean forest: Murder in Myrtle Beach / by Troy D. Nooe.
p. cm.
ISBN 978-1-932158-91-5 (trade pbk. : alk. paper)
1. Private investigators--Fiction. 2. World War,
1939-1945--Veterans--Fiction. 3. Murder--Investigation--Fiction.
4. Myrtle Beach (S.C.)--Fiction. I. Title.
PS3614.O64O34 2011
813'.6--dc22
2010053613

Acknowledgments

The *Ocean Forest* wouldn't be possible without the input and support of a lot of selfless people who contributed their time, opinions and energy into improving what I was working on. With that in mind I'd like to give special thanks:

To Dad for his early edits and research.

To baby sis Laura for her behind the scenes work on the internet.

To John Buntemeyer and Melissa Koz for being my first guinea pigs

To Dino Thompson for sharing his stories and memories and to Jack Thompson for his recollections and wonderful photographs. Both of these men were instrumental in bringing the Ocean Forest Hotel to life for me

To Holland Grayson for his knowledge and insight and to Tom Warner of Litchfield Books for his encouragement and advice

To all of my early readers for donating their time, suggestions, encouragement and for being my sounding boards; Audrey, Kristen, Cheeseburger Bill, Ron, Debbie, Rick, Rudy, Billy, Tara, Tom, Desiree, Jessica, Deirdre, Carey, Karina, Michelle, Paul, Kristine, Stacy, Chris, Steve, Brandon, Elena and Momma Gargano ... hope I didn't forget anyone.

To My kids, Emily, Gregory and Andrew for leaving me just enough brain cells to get the job done

To Bob and Barbara Ingalls and Judy Geary of The Ingalls Publishing Group for believing in my project and making it better

To the gang at Foster's Café and my coworkers at the Marriott Grand Dunes for everything

Lastly, to the City of Myrtle Beach for embracing my idea and showing the love

I hope all of you take pride in our baby.

Dedication

For Walter C. Nooe Jr. or, as I usually refer to him, Dad.
I know it's not much considering all you've done for me over
the years but you know how kids are.
And to the memory of The Ocean Forest Hotel.
I wish I could have seen her first hand.

*"You can pick your poison and you can
pick your friends.
You can pick any direction
but you can't pick where you've been"*

Rise and Shine
By Peter Case and Victoria Williams
Performed by Peter Case

Chapter One

You would think I'd be used to it by now but I still hate to see a grown man cry. There's something about a big burley lug breaking down in tears that wrenches at your gut and twists your insides around. It's like sandpaper on your spine.

"I know it's a tough pill to swallow," I said, for lack of anything better to say.

"How could she do this to me?" He was looking up from the 8x10 glossies I'd given him. "After all we've been through … "

I shrugged. "Dames."

"She's not some dame. She's my wife," Wilson replied, tears rolling down his face.

He didn't look like the same guy who strolled into my office ten minutes earlier. No longer was he the scrapping six-foot-four longshoreman with wide shoulders and a barrel chest, his hair cropped in a high and tight. Now he was slouched over in his chair, weak and busted, curled up and staring at photos of the love of his life leaving some dive motel with another man.

"It happens."

"It doesn't happen to me," he answered and his voice crackled under his words.

"You'd be surprised."

He thumbed through the stack of pictures again with thick,

meaty fingers, rummaging through the pile, still not compre-
hending what he was looking at. I could see the disbelief and
shock in his face.

It's not an easy thing to tell a guy that the woman he's married to is running around on him. It down right stinks, but that's
what my clients pay me to do. I figure it's better coming from me
than for him to come home early from work one day and find his
girl in the sack with another man. At least this way a fellow has
options. He's got time to sort things out and figure out what he
wants to do. That other way people tend to get shot, or beat up or
who knows what. That other way people end up in jail.

Maybe, in some twisted way, I perform a public service.
Maybe because of gumshoes like me guys like Wilson get to
salvage what's left of their pathetic lives and move on. That's
what I tell myself, anyway.

"They hang out in a little gin mill around the corner from
the motel," I explained. "I talked to the bartender and he says
they're regulars. They've been going there for years."

"Years?"

I nodded, slow and easy, giving him a chance to take it in.
"It's an old story and, I hate to say, but I see it all the time. As far
as I can figure she met him while you were overseas. It's a pretty
common thing. You were off fighting in the war. She got lonely
and found some companionship. You come home and she's still
got this other guy in her life."

"You're telling me that while I was over fighting in the Pacific
she was back here balling this guy?"

I shrugged again. "What branch did you serve in?"

"Marines."

I should have known. The Marines always keep the haircut
once they come home. They never lose the look.

"How long were you over there?"

"Three years."

"Three years is a long time. A girl can get pretty lonely in
three years."

"And that gives her the right to do this to me?"

"Of course not, I'm just saying—"

"I'm going to kill the bastard."

10

This is where my public service comes into play.

I pulled out a pack of Lucky Strikes and patted one out, offering one to Wilson but he declined. Taking my time, I lit the cigarette and took a deep drag, letting out a thick cloud of smoke that just kind of lingered between us.

"That's certainly one option. He's kind of a scrawny fellow. I'm guessing you could tear him apart with your bare hands, a big guy like you. Of course you could shoot him, stab him or beat him to death with a baseball bat.

"The problem is they tend to hang people for stuff like that. Now, I don't know this girl of yours but I'm guessing she's not worth dying for."

"She cheated on me."

"True enough but that doesn't mean you can go around killing people. I'll let you in on a little secret—crimes of passion, they don't exist. It's a myth. Murder is murder and it doesn't matter if you commit it in the name of love or greed, it's all the same.

"The fact that you found out like this makes it premeditated. That's Murder One. That's the death penalty. "

"So, what, I should sit back and take it?"

"I didn't say that. You've got options. There's no need to go and do anything rash. The way I see it, you could go home and throw all her stuff into the street. Kick her out, let Romeo take over paying her bills. Cut your ties and be done with her."

"But I still love her," he said, all frail and timid.

"Maybe you need to tell her that. Maybe, instead of busting heads, you could sit down and talk to her. Tell her you know what's what and you're willing to give her another chance but she's got to lose the boyfriend. Tell her you want to try and start fresh."

"You think?"

I shrugged again. I shrug a lot in my business.

"In this racket I see this sort of thing all the time and I'll let you in on another little secret. These flings, these affairs, they hardly ever have anything to do with love or sex. Most of the time, these women are just looking for attention. They find some clown who gives them the time of day and the next thing you know they're swept off their feet."

"You really think it would work?"

11

"It's worth a try. If not, you can always toss her out in the street."

So, I give this guy I just met about a week ago my nickel's worth of advice and I sit back and watch as he soaks it in. As far as I know I might be totally off base but what the hell? It's not like they prepared us for this in the six week course I took at the Staley School of Private Investigation.

Actually, it's not like they prepared us for much of anything that pertained to the job at the Staley School. The only reason I even signed up for the course was because it was covered by the GI Bill. That and the fact I figured the certificate hanging in my office would look good and lend me a certain amount of credibility.

This job is nothing like I thought it would be. I'm not even sure how I ended up here. The only thing I am sure is I'm in no way qualified to be doing this for a living. I'm certainly not qualified to be giving life advice to lugs like Wilson.

After I got out of the service I toyed with the idea of going back to the docks like my old man, like Wilson. My father worked the waterfront all his life and I was on my way to doing the same. I dropped out of high school at sixteen and got into the ILA, went to work on the docks. If it weren't for the war I'd probably still be there.

I took some shrapnel to the leg at Omaha Beach and got shipped home. It looked like I was on my way back to the water-front but something inside me wouldn't let me do it. I guess after seeing the world and living on the edge I couldn't go back to the nine to five. Maybe I was looking for some sort of adventure.

Needless to say, so far, as a private investigator, I hadn't found it.

You probably think that the life of a private dick is full of adventure. Before I got into it, I know I did. I thought it was going to be like the Bogart movies, with beautiful women and damsels in distress, murder cases and kidnappings that I would solve. It's not like that at all. It's not even close.

Most of my cases involve spying on cheating spouses and hiding in the shadows, watching other people live their lives, busting my ass to make the monthly rent on a one room downtown office on the seedy side of Baltimore Street. That's not actually true. Both sides of downtown Baltimore Street are seedy.

Hell, I've taken on cases to find lost dogs to try and make ends meet, anything for a buck. They forgot to tell us about that at the Staley School.

If I were Wilson I would tell me to go jump in a lake. Who am I to give anybody advice? I've never even had a relationship last more than a couple of months. I'm the last person on earth that ought to be telling anybody anything. If Wilson had half a brain in his head he would punch me in the mouth and tell me to mind my own business.

Instead, he pulls out fifty bucks and sets it on my desk. After all, I've got a certificate on my wall that says I know what I'm talking about. He takes the pictures of his wife with her lover and leaves without another word. Wilson looks smaller as he walks out my door.

For a few minutes after he left, I sat puffing on my Lucky Strike and staring down at the money he left me. The bills were crisp and new, like he just went to the bank before he came to see me, but they seemed somehow dirty to me, like they'd been stained by the sins of an entire city.

To me, they looked like they were covered in filth, the kind of filth that once you get it on your hands you can never get it off. I'm very familiar with that kind of filth. I deal with it every day. My hands were already stained by it and I knew in my heart that it would never wash off.

I scooped up the money and stuffed it in my pocket. Filthy or not, I needed it. Next, I opened up the drawer of my desk and pulled out a bottle of rotgut whiskey and a glass. I poured myself three fingers and threw it back.

It wasn't that I particularly needed a drink, but it helped me forget the constant throbbing in my leg and, besides, that's what Bogie used to do in the movies. Like it or not, I learned more about being a private eye from Bogie than I ever did at the Staley School. A lot of good that ever did me.

From the corner of my eye I spotted an envelope peeking out from under a stack of mail, most of it bills. I knew what the envelope contained, but I picked it up and opened it anyway.

Inside was my immediate future, not to mention next month's rent money. It was a train ticket and a hotel reservation.

In the morning I was leaving for Myrtle Beach, South Carolina, a far cry from the dirty streets of Baltimore City. Not that I was going off on vacation. Guys like me don't take vacations. Truth be told, I didn't even want to go. I hate the beach. I have ever since that day on the one they called Omaha. If it were up to me I'd never even look at the ocean again, but that wasn't an option.

When your best friend gets married there's an unwritten rule that says you have to be there. When it's the guy who saved your life that rule is written in stone.

Chapter Two

The train brought me into the Myrtle Beach Train Depot, a dinky little thing by Baltimore standards. Long and thin, it wasn't much bigger than your average mechanic's garage and I guessed you could have fit twenty of them into Baltimore's Penn Station, where I had begun my trip. There was a wooden platform running the length of one side where a few people waited to greet friends and loved ones, and it sat across a dirt road from what passed for the downtown district.

By downtown district I mean a few rows of buildings lined across from each other, slapped in the middle of some trees and houses, dirt and sand roads intersecting with paved ones. I was used to the busy streets of Baltimore with their cars and people, streetcars running down the middle of them, fruit and vegetable venders in horse drawn carts working their way down the sides, screaming out the day's specials. Myrtle Beach seemed like the opposite, quiet lazy storefronts, a handful of people meandering about, the occasional car passing by.

Outside the depot was a little cabstand marked Veteran's Cab. Beside it sat a beat up jalopy that looked like it had been rolled over the top and had the roof beat back out with a ball peen hammer. Behind the wheel was a skinny guy in a short sleeved button down shirt reading a newspaper.

"Do you know how to get to the Ocean Forest Hotel?"

The guy laughed. "What kind of question is that?" he asked in a sharp southern twang. "I s'pect near about everybody knows where the Ocean Forest is."

I climbed in the back and waited. The guy seemed to barely notice I was there and went about finishing his article before neatly folding up his newspaper and setting it aside. When he was good and ready, he started the car and we were off, skirting through town and across half finished roads, zigzagging between local businesses and empty lots. The town was sparse and semi deserted, sporadic shops and houses popping up here and there, a thick dense forest wedging in on the outskirts, threatening to overtake what little civilization there seemed to be.

We hung a left onto a two lane thoroughfare that looked like it might be the main road through town and continued up for about three miles before making a right, heading down a paved road cut out of the thick forest.

I'm not sure what I expected the Ocean Forest to look like, but as we came driving up from an angle off to the right, through the dense green foliage, she caught me off guard.

They said she was the finest hotel between Atlantic City and Miami Beach and it showed. She was a grand and opulent structure set out in the middle of nowhere, lush forest surrounding her on three sides and the Atlantic Ocean at her back. She was long and stretched out on the flanks, tall and majestic in the center. To the right was a separate building, some sort of theater with a huge sand parking lot in front of it.

The road intersected with another at a circle and we followed it around, turning in to the right, pulling past an oval patch of vegetation and coming to a stop at the face of the hotel.

There were a dozen or so suitcases and luggage pieces lined up on the ground out front and a few bellmen sorting through them, black men dressed in ties, short sleeved white shirts and dark slacks. One greeted me with a smile as I got out of the taxi and took my bag, placing it in line with the others and taking my name.

In the center, at ground level, was a door under a green and white awning. This, I was told, led to the commerce area and

16

housed a variety of amenities such as a barber shop, beauty salon, drugstore, beach store, a bar and a bowling alley of all things. There was even an indoor pool filled with salt water.

Staircases on either side of the front of the hotel led to a large open air porch furnished with rocking chairs and small tables. I wandered up the nearer set, passing a few relaxing vacationers as I made my way in.

Through the main entry, to the immediate right was the registration desk and I walked over to begin the process of checking in. Behind it stood a pudgy fellow with Coke bottle glasses, his nose buried deep in the large registration in book in front of him.

I cleared my throat in an effort to attract his attention but it failed to evoke even the slightest response. It was the cab driver all over again. These Southerners weren't much on interruptions.

"As I live and breathe. Francis Murray McKeller," a voice shouted from behind me.

I turned around and there was Bradley Chilton. I hadn't seen him in two years and he looked good, tall, tanned and healthy. He was dressed in a perfectly pressed white suit with a black tie.

"My mother doesn't even call me Francis," I lied.

"Good to see you, Frankie." He stepped up and wrapped his arms around me, squeezing me in a strong affectionate hug.

I'm not ashamed to say that I hugged him back hard. This was the guy I had bunked with all through boot camp, the guy I served side by side with in the European Theater. When I got hit with the shrapnel as we were off loading the landing craft, he was the guy who grabbed me by the collar and dragged me up the beach. While the allied forces were busy fighting the Jerries and taking Omaha Beach, bullets and shells flying everywhere, Bradley bandaged my leg and stopped the bleeding. Then he wrapped my arm around his shoulder and carried me up to cover.

He carried my limp ass all day. If it weren't for Bradley Chilton I never would have gotten off that God forsaken beach. Bradley was more than my best friend, he was like my brother.

We let go and backed away, each giving the other the once over.

"You look good," he said.

"You too, for a guy that's about to tie the knot. You're not really going to go through with this, are you? You do know it's not too late to back out?"

I heard someone clear her throat and Bradley stepped aside to reveal a pretty brunette standing behind him. I liked her from the very first. She was a dainty little thing with a fresh and innocent look about her, oozing with domestic possibilities, proper and beautiful. She was exactly the kind of girl I expected Bradley to end up with.

"Allow me to introduce the future Mrs. Chilton." He smiled. "Lucy, this is Frankie."

"The soon to be *ball and chain*," she said with a smile as she stepped forward and hugged me just about as hard as Bradley had. "Bradley has told me so much about you I feel like I already know you."

I'm not a particularly sentimental guy but I have to admit I got a little choked up standing there hugging my buddy's fiancé. It felt good. It felt like family.

"What do you say we get a drink?" Bradley suggested.

"I haven't finished checking in yet."

I'd almost forgotten I was still standing at the front desk, a dumb muck from the streets of Baltimore surrounded by the luxury and comfort of the Ocean Forest.

The place wasn't at all like I imagined it would be. The lobby was wide and open, white walls illuminated with sunlight from the large bay windows that lined its façade and rear. A crystal chandelier hung in the center of the two story room, a huge decadent thing that made me wonder how they got it in. Below it a tasteful collection of overstuffed chairs and sofas, the occasional coffee table adorning their sides and sitting atop imported oriental rugs. On the right and left were carved wooden archways topped with decorative glass transoms, oval half circles with white trim flaring out like rays of light.

It was clean, classy and sophisticated without reaching a level of gaudiness. There was a reserved elegance about it that spoke of Southern grace and a down home beach easiness. The Ocean Forest was nothing like the flea traps I was used to staying in and it was running me a month's rent for the next four days, but how many times does your brother get married?

"If you would just sign here," the bug eyed desk clerk said, acknowledging me for the first time, turning the guest log toward me and handing me a key.

Bradley tossed him a five spot. "Would you see that Mr. McKeller's bags are taken up to his room?"

"Bag," I corrected, pointing to the lone suitcase stuffed with an extra suit, a used tuxedo and the various toiletries I'd need for the weekend. "I tend to travel light."

"As long as you're here, that's all that matters."

The three of us headed downstairs to the hotel bar while a bellman took my bag up to my room. The bar was called the Brookgreen Room, located on the ground level, and it was every bit as elegant as the lobby. There was a hand carved Mahogany bar that ran along the front before hanging a right for a spell and turning to the left, making sort of a sloppy Z. The top had a polish so deep it looked like you could drink it.

Brass stools with leather cushions lined the front, spaced out every few feet. The wall was mirrored with hand carved woodwork, dimly lit with oak shelves running across and filled with bottles of extravagant hooch like I had never seen. It was like I had died and gone to wino heaven.

"Wow," I sighed.

"Not bad for a dry state, huh?"

"Dry state?"The words caused me to panic and I was reconsidering my stay when Bradley smiled and tried to ease my fears.

"Welcome to the Bible Belt. Technically you can serve beer and wine but the hard stuff is supposed to be illegal. Some places, like the Ocean Forest, can get away with it though."

"How do they do that?"

Bradley shrugged. "I guess it pays to have friends in high places. There are a few spots in town that are allowed to serve the good stuff. Most of the ones that aren't do it anyway until they get raided by the sheriff."

"That's fair."

"They'll serve it until they get busted with a slap on the wrist and a fine and usually be back in business in a couple of days."

"You have a hell of a way of doing things down here."

"They don't call it the good ole boy system for nothing."

We bellied up with Lucy in the center, Bradley and I close in at her shoulders. I took off my grey fedora and tossed it on the bar. Lucy scooped it up and put it on, tilting it off to the side of her head. I could see how Bradley could fall for her.

She was petite and cute with big green eyes and the face of a movie starlet framed by shiny brown hair she wore straight and off her shoulders, not a strand out of place. Her smile was the kind that could light up a ballpark and everything about her screamed of family, babies and white picket fences. She was thin but curvy, filling out her yellow sun dress with the frilly white collar and she looked athletic and healthy, the kind of woman mugs like me seldom get to see and never get to talk to.

Lucy pulled the brim of my hat down low on her face and lifted her chin in the air, peering up at me from under the over-sized fedora. It made her look even smaller and younger.

"What do you think? Do I look a like a detective?"

"I'm going to have to go with no. You're much too pretty."

"You know, I've never actually met a real life private eye."

"Neither have I."

"You must tell me some stories about the cases you work on. I'm dying to know what it's like."

"It's funny you should say that because I'm certain if I told you about what I do it would absolutely bore you to death."

"Bradley ..." She laughed. " You didn't tell me your friend was so funny."

"It's news to me," he replied. "I don't recall Frankie ever having a sense of humor. He must have acquired it back in Baltimore."

"When I'm not doing detective work I have a night club act that I'm working on."

"You are full of surprises, Frankie."

"I'm full of something." I joked.

"What's your poison?"

"Whiskey."

Lucy laughed again. "I would have been so disappointed if you had ordered anything else. It is what detectives are supposed to drink."

"That's what they told us in detective school."

I consider myself a pretty guarded person, tight lipped for the most part. The majority of my conversations take place in my own head and I usually pull both parts. That comes with the territory in my line of work. You need to be able to spend quality alone time with yourself if you're going to do what I do. It probably explains my less than stellar track record when it comes to the fairer sex. Women don't usually enjoy spending time with a guy who sulks and keeps to himself. It tends to put a damper on the whole courtship process.

Something must have snapped in me that day. It was like I was a different person, laughing, joking, and cutting up with a couple of fellow homo-sapiens. I suppose I had always been like that with Bradley. We'd hit it off from the first time we met, and I always felt comfortable around him. He was always able to bring out a side of myself I didn't get to exercise very often.

Bradley Chilton was from old Southern money. I'm talking pre-civil war money with the plantations and slaves and the whole bit. His ancestors had been generals and politicians during the war. My ancestors had been there too but mine were the Mick grunts trudging through the mud and manning the front lines, cannon fodder that fought on the opposite side.

Looking at Bradley now, it wasn't hard to see the aristocratic bloodline that ran through him. He measured in at about six two, handsome with blondish hair and squared features. Intelligent blue eyes and a confident smile made him appear almost stand offish until he opened his mouth to speak in that slow southern drawl that reminded you of American royalty. From there on out he was friendly, laid back and inviting, funny and interesting, generous to a fault. I was a good six years older than Bradley but I always felt like his kid brother.

He'd gone to some Ivy League prep school before the war broke out. Once it hit he'd wanted to join the effort but his father forbade it, wanting him to stay in school. In typical Bradley style, he'd gone behind his father's back and joined anyway, becoming a grunt in the Army like me.

With his father's connections, he could have done anything in the service, rear echelon, an officer, an aid to some big shot

21

General. That wasn't the way Bradley worked, he believed in getting his hands dirty. He wanted to do his part and he wanted to make a difference despite his father's objections.

Even in the service he stood out from the rest of us. Covered in mud and dirt, wearing the same Army drab fatigues as all the other muggs, he always hovered above the crowd. Even the officers could see it, and when they spoke to him they used different voices than they reserved for us peons. Nobody ever talked down to Bradley, no matter what their rank. They were always polite and respectful when speaking to Private Chilton.

Sitting at the bar of the Ocean Forest Hotel, two years and three months since I had last seen him, we picked up from exactly where we left off, and it was like we hadn't seen each other in days. You're lucky if you can count friends like that on one finger.

Lucy wasn't much different. Although I had just met her, I felt like I'd known her forever. There was a relaxing quality to her voice that immediately put you at ease and made you feel like you could open up with anything to her. She was smart and feisty with a sharp sense of humor and a quick tongue but a generous spirit that could soothe a charging rhino. If she were engaged to anybody else on the planet I might have been jealous.

We spent the next hour and five shots of the smoothest bourbon I'd ever tasted catching up. Bradley was working for his father in real estate development, which he didn't seem too thrilled about. He mentioned that he was thinking about branching out on his own as he had big plans for his future. Knowing Bradley the way I did, I had no doubt that he would.

Lucy had been some sort of gymnast in college, which accounted for her athletic physique and I got the feeling that her schooling had been more a formality, preparing her for marriage. She didn't have a job, but she volunteered with some organization dedicated to the preservation of wildlife. It had something to do with environmental conservation and the preservation of wetlands, guarding the natural habitats of South Carolina's indigenous animal life. I had never heard of anything like it and it seemed a bit silly to me. After all, with all the open land across South Carolina and the U. S., I couldn't imagine a time when any animal species might be in danger of actually going extinct. Women will be women, I suppose.

"Lucy fancies herself another Teddy Roosevelt. If it were up to her, she'd turn the entire wilderness into National Parks and wouldn't allow anyone to build anything anywhere."

"Nonsense, I'm just trying to look out for those who can't look out for themselves."

"Well, you might want to look out for us while you're at it. Don't forget that I happen to be in the real estate business and I'm rather fond of eating, you know."

"So, what's the plan for the weekend?" I asked.

"We take the plunge in three days," Bradley answered. "Tonight it's cocktails and dinner with family and friends, tomorrow we spend the day on the beach…"

"I hope you brought your swimsuit," Lucy cut in.

"I'm not much of a beach guy. The last time I was on a beach it wasn't one of my luckiest days."

"As I remember, it was an extremely lucky day for you. It could have been a lot worse."

"Well, it was lucky for me that you were there."

Lucy glanced back and forth to both of us. "What exactly happened on that day? Bradley plain refuses to talk about it."

I looked over to Bradley and him at me. We both fell silent in that way veterans tend to do when such topics come up. Lucy looked baffled so I thought maybe I should throw her a bone.

"Your fiancé saved my life." She deserved to know that much.

"As always, my imaginative friend has a tendency to exaggerate. I merely gave him a little boost in much the way I did all through boot camp and the rest of the war, for that matter."

The master of understatement and modest to boot, Bradley played it off to a T and it was obvious that it wasn't the time or the place to go into further detail. It was yet another reason I loved Bradley Chilton.

The truth of the matter is what he did that day was nothing short of heroic and if there were any justice in the world he would have received a medal for it. Unfortunately for him, if they were to give medals to everyone who did something heroic on that beach that day there wouldn't be enough medals to go around. I guess, in a way, I was Bradley Chilton's medal.

"Like I was saying, tomorrow it's fun and sun in the sand, followed by an extremely pretentious, and I'm sure, very boring dinner. Then it's one more day until the happy nuptials. "

Lucy giggled. "At least you said happy nuptials this time. With all this talk of tying knots and taking plunges I was beginning to think you were having a change of heart."

Bradley leaned in and gave her a light kiss on the cheek. "Don't be silly. I've been a fisherman long enough to know a keeper when I see one."

"So now I'm an old fish, am I? The way you speak to me it's a wonder I ever agreed to marry you."

"I've wondered about that myself. That's why I'm pushing to marry you so quick, before you come to your senses." They kissed again, this time a long soft kiss to the lips.

I turned back to my drink, feeling a bit like a third wheel. It was almost embarrassing to be there, like I was witnessing something that was meant to be private and personal. You would think I'd be used to that sort of thing in my line of work.

My thoughts turned to Wilson the longshoreman and his estranged wife and to the dozens of other clients I'd had over the last two years. I wondered how many of them had begun their lives together in much the same way as Lucy and Bradley. I wondered how many of them had started out as loving and romantic before the world came crashing in on them and turned their lives to hell. It made me hate my job even more.

Chapter Three

The party broke up not long after and I found my way up to my room for a quick cat nap before dinner. The five shots of Kentucky's finest had made me a little drowsy, and I figured I should sleep it off as best I could before facing Bradley and Lucy's old money family and friends.

A room at the Ocean Forest was like nothing I had ever seen before or since and I began to understand why it cost as much as it did. Anything its size would have housed two families in my old neighborhood and the bed was large enough for me and a Packard. I was afraid if I fell asleep and rolled over to the other side of those satin sheets I might wake up in another time zone.

The place was beyond fancy with velvet curtains, brass fixtures and antique upholstered furniture. Intricate woodwork ordained the walls where normal people put molding and there was a bureau with enough space to house my entire wardrobe and forget where I put it. Beside the bed was a crystal water pitcher with matching glasses and the tub featured not only hot and cold but running salt water as well. I couldn't help but wonder if there were actually people who lived like this on a daily basis.

I managed about an hour of shut eye before dragging myself

out of bed and going about the tedious chore of getting into my penguin outfit. I'd brought it down stuffed in a suitcase so before I laid down for my nap I laid it out between the mattress and box spring, hoping to press out the wrinkles. For the record, it's not the most effective method for pressing tuxedos.

I was fidgeting with my collar and pulling at my jacket the whole way down in the elevator while the operator kept giving me strange looks. He was a freckled-faced sixteen-year-old who looked like he'd rather be somewhere else. I knew the feeling.

As I mentioned earlier, the tuxedo I bought was second hand but it didn't look it. It didn't look it until I stepped off the elevator, walked into the lobby and saw what everyone else was wearing, anyway, and then it looked third hand.

The hotel had set up a small reception area off to the side of the lobby complete with a bar and an hors d'oeuvres table where the wedding guests could gather and mingle before dinner. The area was filled with extremely well dressed people standing around in groups chatting.

I made a beeline to the bar and ordered a whiskey neat with a water chaser. There was no charge as it was a very classy affair, first class all the way. The whiskey had just burned its way down my throat when someone behind me said, "Two fisted, I like that."

When I turned around, with a shot glass in one hand and water glass in the other, I almost choked on my drink. Standing before me was the most exquisite example of the female form I had ever laid eyes on.

While Lucy was beautiful and lovely, wholesome and fresh, this woman was a whole different ballgame. If it had been a movie, Lucy would have been the leading lady, the love interest, the nice girl. This woman would be something else, the seductress or vixen, the one who convinces some sap to knock off his brother with a bat of her eyes. She was the kind of dame who didn't know what it was like to be the second prettiest girl in a room.

She was tall and proper, on the thin side of plump with curves that flowed into tomorrow and smacked you in the face like a wet towel. Her gown was long and white, held up by thin straps that draped over her perfect shoulders, and it shimmied down her body in ripples accentuating every morsel of her figure.

The face wasn't bad either. Sun bleached blonde hair hung around it, straight in the back and sides but slightly curled at the edges, twisting out this way and that. Her eyes were dark and bright at the same time and set under arched brows, perfectly groomed like they had been painted on by an artist. Every contour of her face was flawless, flowing together like pieces of some angelic puzzle, high cheekbones, moist red lips and a strong but feminine jaw line. Her skin was smooth and the color of moonlight, the cheeks slightly flushed.

"I'm Katherine," she said, holding out her hand for me to take. "Katherine Mathews."

I took it lightly and held it in my finger tips. "Katherine," I repeated.

We both stood there for what must have seemed an awkwardly long time. I couldn't take my eyes off her.

"And should I guess who you might be?" she asked in a sweet southern accent that reminded me of springtime.

Finally, I shook myself out of the trance she'd placed me in. "Frankie," I said. "Frankie McKeller."

"Nice to meet you, Frankie McKeller."

"Likewise."

"I would not be opposed to your buying me a drink," Katherine said, glancing to the bar.

"There's nothing to buy. It's all free."

She laughed slightly, bringing her hand to her lips. "I know, it was meant to be a joke."

The slush was starting to seep out of my brain and I managed to pull myself together. I ordered her a drink; something called a mint julep, and handed it to her. She took the smallest of sips and cocked her head a little to the side.

"Bride or groom?"

"Excuse me?" In my tattered state, I thought, at first, she was asking me to marry her. I was prepared to say yes.

"Who are you here with, the bride or groom?"

"Oh, the groom, I'm a friend of Bradley's. We were in the Army together."

Katherine glanced up like she was searching above me for

some lost piece of information. "I know who you are. You're some sort of police officer or something."

"Not quite. I'm a private detective."

"How exciting."

"Not really, I'm afraid."

She took another sip, this one even smaller, as we both stood in silence, her blushing slightly and me burning holes in her face with my eyes.

"Are you here with anyone?" I finally asked. "A husband or a fiancé?"

"My, aren't you forward?" She blushed a little more.

"It's just that I don't want to be attacked from behind by some jealous boyfriend for talking with you."

"You're quite safe in that regard."

"Katherine," someone said, and an elderly rotund man pushed his way past me to plant a kiss on her cheek. "It's so good to see you." He was a bloated sort of guy with a smooth head and no neck, squinty eyes and a look on his face like someone was pinching him from behind.

"Mr. Chilton, allow me to introduce you to Frankie McKeller," she said, nudging him around to me. "Frankie and Bradley served together in the war."

Bradley's father gave me a hard look and let out a huff. In his defense, I think it had more to do with the mention of the war than anything to do with me.

"That confounded war. I never approved of him going off like that."

I nodded, not sure how to answer.

"I suppose it all turned out for the best. You both made it back in one piece. There's something to be said for that."

"There is that," I agreed.

Just then, another man reached across me and put his hand on Chilton's shoulder. This guy was of average height with a beak like nose, receded graying hair and wire rimmed glasses. There was something nervous and jittery about his appearance. "Mr. Chilton, I need to speak with you," he said, paying no attention to Katherine or myself.

"Can't it wait, Tucker?"

"Well … it's just that … I've come into the possession of certain information, Sir."

Chilton ignored the man and looked at me. "Tucker here has been a fine assistant for years but he has a little trouble leaving business at the office." Then to Tucker, "In case you haven't noticed, my only son is getting married this weekend."

"Yes Sir, I realize that but it's just—"

Chilton cut him off. "Mr. McKeller here served with Bradley during the war."

Tucker turned to me. "Is that so?" he asked, looking at me with what looked a lot like suspicion. He reached out and shook my hand, telling me it was a pleasure to meet me but he didn't sound very convincing before turning back to Chilton. "If I could just have a moment of your time, Sir—"

"It will have to wait, Tucker."

"Yes Sir but—"

"We will discuss the matter at a later time," the old man snapped in a tone that made it clear that it was no longer open for discussion.

"Yes Sir." Tucker slinked away.

"A fine employee but a bit overzealous at times, I'm afraid."

It didn't seem to be the kind of statement that required a response.

"Well, just the same, very nice to meet you," the old man offered.

"You too." We shook hands briefly and the elderly Chilton went on his way.

"Nice gent," I said with a touch of sarcasm in my voice.

Katherine laughed a little. "He's not so bad, just stuck in his ways. I'm afraid Bradley has been an utter source of aggravation for him since he was a young boy."

"Well, I know Bradley enlisted against his father's wishes."

Katherine laughed harder and covered her mouth with the back of her hand in an attempt to keep what she was saying between us. "Bradley has made a lifetime career of going against his father's wishes. The two are like water and oil."

"That must make it tough to work together."

"I certainly wouldn't want to spend any time in that office

29

with the two of them."

"What's the old man going to do when Bradley goes off on his own?"

Katherine grabbed me by the arm and leaned in close and the sweet scent of her made me dizzy. "Heavens don't say such a thing out loud. Old man Chilton would cancel the wedding if he even thought Bradley was considering leaving the firm. Why, he already threatens to cut him off completely about every other month."

"I'm guessing that Bradley will do OK for himself."

"Bradley will be just fine. He knows exactly what he's doing. Bradley has a plan for himself."

"You seem like you're firmly in the loop here."

She gave me a smile that would melt a lesser man. It did a pretty good number on me. "I grew up with all these people. I went to school with Bradley and Lucy. We played together as kids."

"So, what you're telling me is, you're filthy rich."

"Hardly, my family was one of the wealthier families in the area for years, but I'm afraid my dearly departed father made some rather poor business investments over the last few years of his life.

"No, I'm one of the ones that the others look at and say 'poor little Katherine'." She said it matter of fact, like it was some sort of joke.

I glanced down at the dress she was wearing, the diamond necklace across her perfect neck, and the gold bracelet on her thin wrist. "You don't look so poor."

"I'm not destitute, if that's what you mean. We still have the house and some holdings and quite a bit of land in the area but I'm afraid it's mostly swampland, not very valuable. Besides, this is the South, Mr. McKeller, appearances are everything."

"As far as appearances go, I'd say you're pulling that off just fine."

Katherine blushed a little again and took another sip of her mint julep. "All things considered, I can't complain. My family has fared better than some. Take Lucy, for example. Her father lost pretty much everything. About all they have left is a track of swampland."

"I met her earlier. She doesn't seem too broken up about it."

"Well, it's not all about money now, is it?"

"Not until you don't have any."

"Why, Mr. McKeller, all this time I thought you were some kind of romantic, the way you've been carrying on, but I do believe that you're a cynic."

"You have no idea," I told her. "And, for the record, I liked it better when you called me Frankie."

Chapter Four

*T*he newlyweds to-be made it to the reception just before we were to go into dinner, a grand entrance complete with applause and accolades. I had just enough time to take Bradley aside.

"How's this dinner thing work?"

"It's pretty simple, they put food in front of you and you eat it," Bradley responded in smart ass style.

"That I get. I'm talking about the seating arrangements. Is it assigned seating?"

"Yes, there will be a place card with your name on it."

"Any chance you can get me switched around; get me seated next to Katherine Mathews?"

Bradley stopped and gave me a funny look. "Katherine?"

"Yeah, pretty blonde, you grew up with her?"

"I know *who* she is, I just want to know why?"

"Gee, that's a tough one. Pretty girl, cute figure, nice smile ... "

"Well, sure, but—"

"Look, if it's a problem, forget it."

"No, of course not, I'll take care of it."

"Thanks buddy. I appreciate it."

That's how I happened to be seated next to Katherine at dinner.

"Fancy meeting up with you again," I said as she strolled up to her seat.

"You detectives seem to be quite resourceful," she replied with a smile as I pulled out her chair and held it for her to take, pushing it back in as she sat. It looked like she was still nursing the same mint julep I'd gotten her earlier.

The crowd was settling in to their seats, preparing for dinner. We were on the south wing of the hotel and in the main ballroom of the Ocean Forest. This room was so nice it made the rest of the hotel look dingy, if that were possible.

It was gigantic and dimly lit. The walls were done in velvet and hardwood with Roman style pilasters built in at various intervals. The floor was polished marble and there were twenty or so tables spread across it, each adorned with white linen tablecloths and set with fine china plates, crystal glasses and sterling silver utensils. A string quartet was plucking and strumming away on the large stage at the rear of the room and in the center of the ceiling was the largest chandelier I'd ever seen with smaller ones spread around it, like planets orbiting the sun.

Waiters in white dinner jackets and black ties went about filling our water glasses and taking our drink orders. I ordered my usual.

Our table was off to the left of the head table where Bradley and Lucy sat with their parents. Katherine gave me the lowdown.

"Of course, you met Mr. Chilton; next to him is his wife." The older woman in question was gray haired, thin and boney, dressed in a sequined gown with long earrings dangling at the side of her head. Her hair was piled high, swirled around like some sort of cocoon hat and she sat rigid, staring off in front of her, seemingly oblivious to what was going on around her.

"Word is that Mrs. Chilton suffers from severe rheumatism and her doctors have prescribed a regiment of sedatives to relieve her discomfort. As a result, she seldom ventures out in public and is even more seldom anywhere close to coherent."

"Mommy's a hop head?"

"Lord no, Mr. McKeller, everyone knows we don't have

such types in South Carolina. Mrs. Chilton is merely an unfortunate victim of circumstance doing her best to cope with her condition."

"What happened too calling me Frankie?"

She gave me a look. "When I was growing up, Frankie, Mrs. Chilton was the dearest soul I'd ever met, I loved her so. I see her quite often but I haven't spoken with her in years. I'm not sure she's still capable."

"What about Lucy's clan?"

Next to Lucy sat a stoic looking man, tall and thin, with thick dark hair and beady eyes. He sat erect with his head held high and his chin raised. I had never seen a picture of Abraham Lincoln's father but I imagine he might have looked a lot like Lucy's old man. Her mother was small and a bit on the dumpy side. She had a short, sensible haircut and round face. Aside from the happy couple, she was the only one smiling at the table and she had soft, friendly eyes that reminded me of her daughter's.

"Herbert and Lydia Fleming," Katherine informed me, "sweet people but seriously old fashioned. The mother's nice enough but loves to talk. She's always up on the latest gossip and likes nothing better than go on for hours on end. She's not the person you want to get caught in a conversation with; she can literally talk your ear off."

"A woman who likes to talk? That's a new one."

Katherine ignored my remark. "Herbert Fleming is a true piece of work, something straight out of the Victorian Age. Proud and stubborn, he refuses to admit that he and his family are in dire straits financially. All in all, he's lost pretty much everything, but you'd never know it to talk to him. For years he has lived on the generosity of friends and family, selling off everything he can to keep afloat."

"Everything but that track of swampland?"

"He'd sell that too if he could find a buyer."

"It's all about keeping up appearances," I reminded her.

"Talk about a new one, a man who actually listens to what a woman says."

"You're a hard woman not to pay attention to."

"How you do flirt." She laughed.

"What's your story, no rich boyfriends or millionaire suitors? I would think they'd be knocking the door down to court a woman like you."

"Are you always so forward?" she asked, giggling into her palm and blushing.

"No, actually I'm not."

"Well then, I guess I should be flattered."

"That's kind of what I was going for. Now back to the question."

"I've had my share of suitors over the years but I'm afraid I was spoken for most of my life. At the moment I happen to be recovering from a tremendous heartbreak." She said it lightly and it didn't seem remotely believable.

"What kind of knucklehead would let a girl like you get away?"

Katherine looked at me with unsure eyes like she was trying to size me up. "Are you playing with me?"

"Why would I do something like that?"

"You really don't know?"

"I'm new in town."

She looked around, making sure that no one was listening and leaned in toward me. "Up until about six months ago, I was engaged to Bradley."

Talk about your cold slap in the face. The words didn't even make sense. My eyes instinctively shot up to the head table and locked on to my best friend. He was looking back at me with what could only be described as concern.

"You and Bradley?"

"Bradley and I were high school sweethearts. Most everyone around just assumed that it would be me up there becoming the next Mrs. Chilton. It was an absolute scandal when he broke it off."

"Gee, you think you know a guy."

"It's all for the best. Lucy is a lovely girl and I'm sure they'll be very happy." I detected a cold tone in her voice when she said it like she was trying to convince both of us it were true.

"I had no idea."

"You can't do that!" someone yelled and the whole place went

35

silent. Three tables over, a man stood with his hands clenched in fists, glaring down at another man.

The guy sitting, who had just taken the brunt of the shouting, was the weasely Tucker fellow I had met earlier. The chap hovering over him was young and muscular, with reddish hair and an even redder face. He suddenly realized the entire ballroom was looking at him and relaxed his stance, smiling with embarrassment. After saying something to Tucker under his breath, he turned and walked away.

"What was that all about?" I asked Katherine.

"I have no idea."

"What's the deal on Tucker?"

"Tucker Morgan, he's been working for Mr. Chilton for years, long before the war even. He was Mr. Chilton's right hand man until Bradley joined the firm."

"And the other guy?"

"Gilbert Fleming, Lucy's brother."

"Does he always cause scenes at these gatherings?"

"Gilbert doesn't often attend these gatherings. He has a bit of a wild streak in him. I guess you could say that he's kind of the black sheep of the family."

"The black sheep in a family that's had the rug pulled out from under them, interesting."

"Gilbert is what you would call the playboy type. You name it and he probably does it, drinking, gambling, running around with women of ill repute ..."

"Mr. Fleming must love that, what with his Victorian values and all."

"I believe that Herbert Fleming is more embarrassed about Gilbert than he is about losing all his money."

"So, how does Gilbert manage to maintain a lifestyle like that if his family has gone belly up?"

"That's a good question. Gilbert has always lived above his means but I don't know how he manages it. They say that he's a bit of a flim-flam man, always getting involved with all sorts of crazy schemes and crooked deals."

I glanced back up at the head table. Bradley was no longer looking in my direction. Now he was staring over at Gilbert

Fleming who had made his way back to his own table. The look he was giving him was much more than the concern I had seen when he was looking at me. This was a look of pure anger. In-laws can do that to you, even future in-laws.

"Tell me, Frankie, where you come from, do they have such soap operas and goings on?" Katherine asked me and the dark pupils of her eyes looked as big as saucers.

I thought of home and I thought of the many clients that had passed through my office door. I thought of all the lies and deceit I had witnessed, of all the times I had followed men and women to seedy motels and rundown apartment buildings, trying to catch them in the act. I thought of the spouses who sat at my desk crying, some of them hysterical and destroyed, none of them wanting to believe what I told them. I thought of all the lives I had seen in shambles and the devastation that was left in the wake of marriages and relationships gone sour.

"Yeah," I said to her, still lost somewhere in her gaze, trying to get a read on this beautiful woman who used to be engaged to my best friend. "We get some of that up there too."

Chapter Five

The dinner had been nothing short of the best dining experience of my life. They started off with an appetizer they called shrimp cocktail, five boiled shrimp perched on the rim of a glass filled with a concoction of ketchup and horse radish sauce. Next, they served us a bowl of something called She Crab Soup which is a cream based soup loaded with crab meat, sweet and heavenly. The main course consisted of a filet of beef so tender you could eat it with a spoon and a lobster tail, which I had never tried before. For a guy whose diet usually consisted of char grilled burgers from a greasy spoon it was a near religious experience. They served cheesecake for dessert. If you've never had cheesecake before, I suggest you drop whatever you're doing and run out and get some.

The conversation with Katherine had been light and fun loving; I even managed to get a few words in edgewise between woofing down my chow. She continued to amaze me with her wit and perception, incredible beauty aside she had a personality and way about her that caught me off guard.

I had known a lot of women back in Baltimore, but I had never met a woman like Katherine Mathews. She was the complete package and it was difficult for me to comprehend that she belonged to the same gender as the women I spied on and followed to sleazy motels. She was above all that.

After dinner we retired to the terrace out back for cocktails and conversation in the moonlight, the ocean off behind us another hundred yards or so. It was the post dinner reception.

Katherine wandered off to mingle with friends and, although it physically hurt to see her go, I made my way through the room. My leg was aching and I threw down a couple more shots of whiskey to ease the pain. By this point, constant pain in my bum leg was just a way of life and I had learned to live with it.

"How was dinner?" Bradley asked me, breaking away from another conversation as he saw me approach. Lucy was on his arm.

"Not half bad."

"We realize that we don't have the fine cuisine of a big city like Baltimore but we try to make do with what we have."

"You guys in South Cackalaki keep trying, you'll get it right one of these days."

"How was the company?" Lucy asked. "I hope Katherine didn't bore you too much."

"Not at all, she was very charming."

"Katherine is a sweet girl," Lucy replied and I could sense a tinge of animosity in her voice. Knowing what I did, it didn't seem too surprising.

"How is your brother doing? Is everything all right with that?"

Lucy looked a little stunned at the mention of her sibling. "Of course, Gilbert is just a little high strung at times; it was nothing."

I gave my signature shoulder shrug. "Family, what are you going to do?"

"So, what did you two talk about?" Bradley asked.

"A little bit of everything." I replied, as noncommittal as possible.

Speak of the devil; Gilbert Fleming interjected himself into our circle. "Hi kids, how's it treating you?"

Introductions were made, hands were shook. He seemed like a good enough bloke, friendly and out going, personable and confident. Somewhere in the background, everyone seemed a bit uneasy.

"So, you're the guy that got Bradley through World War Two," he said.

"I think it was the other way around."

"Those nips in the Philippines are lucky it wasn't me over there. I would have let them have it good," he said, patting his side quick where a gun holster might be and whipping out a dangerous looking forefinger and thumb. From there he began pointing it around the room, popping off invisible rounds. "Rat-atat-tat. I would have got my share, that's for sure."

I had met my share of Monday morning quarterbacks in my time but Gilbert Fleming was my first Monday morning war hero.

"Yeah, lucky for them you were back here, huh?"

Gilbert shot me an undisguised sneer. "I would have been there too, if it weren't for these darned fallen arches of mine."

"Tough break."

"Say, bud, what's that crack supposed to mean?" It looked like I hit a nerve.

"Not a thing, just making an observation."

Gilbert hesitated for a moment, giving me the once over and sizing me up. "I'll have you know that I was working on some very important stuff during the war, top secret government stuff I'm not at liberty to talk about. If I could, I'd tell you some stories."

"I bet you would." My read on Gilbert Fleming was getting clearer by the second. The guy was a loud mouth and a braggart and I doubted you could take anything he said without at least a grain of salt. I'd met worse.

"Just the same, so glad you could make it down for the wedding." His voice had lost some of the friendly it had when he approached.

"I wouldn't miss it for the world."

He turned to Bradley. "I need to talk to you about something."

Bradley nodded. "Of course."

The two of them wandered off and I was left alone with Lucy. There are worse places a guy could find himself in.

"Are you getting nervous?" I asked, making small talk.

Lucy beamed. "Not at all. I couldn't be happier. This is what

I've dreamed of for years." I had her attention but I couldn't help but notice she kept glancing off toward the direction Bradley and her brother had gone.

"He's quite a guy."

Lucy just smiled.

"He's quite a lucky guy too."

"Thank you," she replied, soft and sincere, still glancing back past me for a glimpse of her brother and fiancé.

From there it was chit chat followed by a couple more shots of bourbon. Since that morning I had taken a train to South Carolina, spent the evening in a swank hotel and had the most luxurious dinner of my life. Much of the night had involved me being on my feet, and my leg was killing me. Even the whiskey wasn't helping anymore. I endured it as long as I could but finally decided it was time to give it a rest.

I had to excuse myself and call it a night. I limped back to the elevator and the freckled face operator took me back up to the third floor where I was staying. He looked at me just as funny as he had on the way down. Maybe it was all in my head.

Off the elevator, I hobbled my way down the hallway, cringing with every step I took and dreaming of collapsing into that luxurious bed. At my door, I was fumbling with my key when I heard voices from the other end of the hallway.

Six or seven rooms down were Tucker Morgan and Gilbert Fleming standing outside of another room. Apparently, they were continuing the argument they had begun earlier. Their gestures spoke volumes and I didn't have to hear what they were saying to know that they were in the midst of a heated conversation.

Gilbert seemed on the offensive, but Tucker was holding his own and looked to be standing his ground with the bigger man. Part of me was curious as to what was going on, but the pain in my leg had become almost unbearable and my first and foremost thoughts were of getting off my feet. I ignored the impulse to go down and try to diffuse the situation.

Whatever was going on had nothing to do with me, and the only thing I wanted was to climb into bed. I unlocked my door, ripped off my monkey suit and collapsed in my rack. Despite the pain that was gnawing my leg, I passed out in minutes.

Chapter Six

*I*t's a funny thing about gunshots. They'll wake you up out of a sound sleep and snap you back to reality like nothing else on earth. I'd heard quite a few in my day. That afternoon on Omaha Beach I'd heard enough to last a lifetime. But it didn't make the one at the Ocean Forest Hotel that night any less dramatic.

I jumped out of bed in a fog and fumbled to climb into a terry cloth bathrobe. Not that I actually owned one but the Ocean Forest was kind enough to supply one for all its guests.

Running out in the hallway, I tried to clear the sleep from my brain and figure out what was going on. A crowd was gathering in the corridor. People tend to migrate toward bad things.

Instinctively, I moved toward the direction the noise had come from and found myself heading down the hallway, to the door I had seen Gilbert Fleming and Tucker Morgan arguing in front of. The door was open and there were people standing at the entrance. I pushed my way past and entered the room.

On the floor was the body of what had once been Tucker Morgan. He looked much the same as the last time I had seen him except for the bullet wound to his forehead and the brain matter splattered out the back of his head. I had seen my share of dead bodies too, but it didn't make the sight of Tucker Morgan lying on the floor with his brains blown across the room any less repulsive.

"What's going on here?" Old man Chilton came storming into the room.

I glanced around to all the people standing about. I was struck by the fact we were all wearing matching bathrobes.

"Somebody needs to call the police," I said with authority, like I had a clue what to do.

"What's happened here?" the old man asked.

"Either there's been a murder or your man Tucker was not happy with the accommodations," I said. I can be a complete asshole at times.

Chaos was breaking out in and around the room, women crying, men gasping and a ghoulish sense of curiosity throughout as people paraded by, everyone wanting to get a glimpse of the gruesome scene. It was turning into some kind of morbid carnival. Somebody had to step up.

"Everybody out!" I yelled. "File out the door and nobody touch anything."

For some reason, they listened. People were working their way out the door and holding their arms together and up, careful not to handle anything in the room. Bradley came rushing in, fighting the grain of the exiting crowd.

"What happened?" he asked me.

"Unless Tucker here figured out how to dispose of the weapon after he shot himself, I'd say that someone came in here and killed him." We detectives are perceptive like that.

"Who would do that?" Bradley asked, in the state of shock.

"My guess is it's someone who wasn't very fond of Tucker Morgan." I took my friend by the shoulder and turned him toward the door, guiding him out and leaving the room with him. He resisted at first, but I explained how it's probably a bad idea to stand in the middle of a crime scene. Besides that, it's bad mojo to stand around gawking at dead folks.

The two of us stopped just outside the doorway, keeping guard over the area and making sure no one else entered before the police got there. Bradley was a mess, physically shaken at the sight of Tucker's body.

"Poor chap," he said. "I can't believe someone would shoot

him like that."

"It certainly puts a damper on the festivities."

Others were arriving, most of them coming up and trying to peer past us into the room, all of them asking questions we couldn't answer. We shooed them away as best we could.

"A little respect for the dead," Bradley finally said, reaching back and pulling the door shut in an effort to put a stop to the sight-seeing. I tried to stop him but my reflexes weren't quick enough.

"What?" he asked.

"The doorknob," I explained. "Fingerprints."

Bradley's face went white. "I never thought about that."

"I guess you don't get too many murders down here in paradise."

Katherine came rushing down the hallway. She was wearing a long beige nightgown, satin and clingy. Over it was a thin matching robe, hanging open at the front and untied. Her hair was disheveled and slightly wild, sticking out in every direction.

I couldn't help but study her as she approached, noticing the outline of her long legs through the soft fabric of the gown with every step she took. Following them down, imagining them through the material, down to her small delicate feet.

It was then I noticed something a little odd. The fact that she'd taken the time to put on a robe but not slip into a pair of slippers wasn't it. The kicker for me was her feet. There, as she got closer, I noticed there was some kind of dirt along the tops and in between her toes. As she came up to us I realized it was sand.

"What's all the commotion about?" she asked in a breathless southern drawl.

"It's Tucker Morgan," Bradley explained. "He's been murdered."

"Somebody thought his head wasn't getting enough ventilation," I added, regretting it as soon as I said it.

Katherine looked at me confused, a little repulsed, then over to Bradley.

"He's been shot," Bradley added.

Her eyes went wide with shock, a painful look of horror spreading across her pretty features. "How awful," she panted, stepping into Bradley and collapsing against him as he took her into his arms, consoling her with gentle pats to her back.

At first it seemed a little inappropriate or maybe it was just a touch of jealousy creeping into my psyche. Sure he was engaged to someone else and about to be married but at the same time there was a history between the two. It's not like they were making out in the hallway.

"Bradley?"

From the other direction, Lucy came running up, flushed and out of breath. There was a scared look in her eye and she looked disheveled and rattled. I guess she didn't have gunshots in mind when she envisioned her perfect wedding.

Bradley dropped his hold on Katherine, turning to his fiancé. He raised his hands, beckoning her to join him and she followed suit, taking her place in his embrace as he explained what was going on. Her reaction was much the same as Katherine's.

As I stood watching him pamper Lucy, hugging her, gently caressing her back, I was struck by the thought that some guys have all the luck. For a moment I thought of placing my arms around Katherine in an effort to soothe her in much the way Bradley had, wondering what she would feel like pressed up against me. I let the thought pass.

"Who would do such a thing?" Lucy gasped.

"Has anyone seen Gilbert lately?" I asked.

Lucy pushed herself away from her future husband and whipped around to face me. Those gorgeous green eyes I had found so friendly and inviting were full of fire.

"What's that supposed to mean?"

She caught me off guard and I felt guilty for opening my trap. "Nothing," I tried. "It's just that after last night I'm sure the police are going to want to speak with him."

"My brother is a lot of things and he may have made his share of mistakes over the years but he is not a killer." Lucy's words were sharp and angry.

"Of course, I didn't mean to imply that he was. I was just pointing out that after what happened it might be a good idea if he were to come forward of his own accord. The last thing in the world he would want is for the police to think he was hiding something."

"I can assure you there is nothing to hide. It was one off handed remark at a party. "

One thing I've learned about myself over the years is that I rarely know when to keep my big mouth shut. "Actually, it was a little more than that. I saw the two of them outside this very door last night as I was going back to my room. They didn't seem to be on friendly terms."

"You can't think Gilbert had anything to do with this," Bradley said.

"I don't think anything. I don't even know the guy. I'm just saying, if he doesn't want to be the main suspect in a murder investigation he might not want to lay too low for awhile."

It was about then the police arrived.

Chapter Seven

Sheriff Rufus Talbert of the Myrtle Beach Sheriff's Department was tall and wiry, the kind of guy who gave the impression that you didn't want mix it up with him in a bar fight. A young fifty, he was a no nonsense straight shooter, and when he spoke he expected his words to not only be heard but followed to the letter.

He was leading the Morgan murder investigation, as Myrtle Beach had no homicide division, and he made it clear that he was none too happy about it, as though committing a crime in his town was a personal insult to him. Maybe the fact that he'd been dragged out of bed in the middle of the night had something to do with his bad mood.

Talbert arrived on the scene with three deputies and a pair of ambulance attendants. After going in and inspecting the murder scene, he and two of the deputies came back out into the hallway while the other three took care of the body.

"Anybody want to tell me who the victim is?"

Nobody wanted to be the first to speak up. Bradley finally stepped forward.

"His name is Tucker Morgan."

"And who might you be?"

Bradley explained the situation, who he was, and about why

we were all there, the wedding and what not.

"Who found the body?"

Again people were timid about stepping up. I figured it was my turn.

"It's hard to say who was first. After the shot went off a bunch of us came running. I was one of the first on the scene."

"Who are you?"

"Frank McKeller. I'm a wedding guest."

"Did you see anybody leaving the room?"

I shook my head no.

Sheriff Talbert looked around the crowd. "Anybody see anyone leaving the room?"

Not a peep from the peanut gallery.

"Anybody see anything?"

Again, no one responded.

Talbert pushed his hat up and scratched his head. "It's going to be a long night, folks," he said to no one in particular.

Old man Chilton was coming back down the hall. He'd gone back to his room and changed into a suit. I guess the pajamas and robe weren't dignified enough for the old bird.

"I don't think that will be necessary, officer."

"Oh, you don't, do you?"

"My name is Alfred Chilton of Chilton Real Estate Investments Inc.," the old man boasted. "These people are my guests. I don't see any need to inconvenience them anymore than we already have."

Talbert wrinkled his brow. "No, of course we wouldn't want to inconvenience anyone. What do you say we just forget about the guy in the next room with the slug in his brain?"

Chilton cleared his throat. "That unfortunate soul you refer to was a dear and trusted colleague and employee of mine. I'm certainly not suggesting that we sweep anything under the carpet. I have faith that you and your men will get to the bottom of this tragedy and bring the culprit responsible for this atrocious act to justice."

"Thanks for the boost of confidence," Talbert replied sarcastically.

"I can assure you that we will all cooperate completely with you and your men. It's just that it's been a very long day and we have been through a terrible ordeal. I suggest that we all retire for the night and start anew in the morning."

"Yeah, that's a great idea. In the mean time, the killer can make a break for the state line."

"Officer ... "

"Sheriff," Talbert corrected. "Sheriff Rufus Talbert."

"Of course, Sheriff, could I have a word with you in private?"

The two went off down the hall a ways until they were out of earshot from the rest of us. Their talk lasted less than five minutes. I can only guess that Chilton was doing some serious name dropping, filling the good sheriff in about his golf outings with the mayor and lunches with the governor.

When they came back Talbert looked more irritated than ever. "After discussing the situation with Mr. Chilton, I've decided to let everyone go to bed for the night. We're going to need to get everyone's name and room number before you're released.

"And just so everyone knows, anyone attempting to leave the building before being interviewed by myself or my deputies will be considered a prime suspect in this case and a fugitive from the law. We will begin questioning in the morning. I'll have men posted at all the exits in case anybody gets any bright ideas."

We all lined up in front of the officers and prepared to give our information. For some reason it seemed like a good idea for me to get in Talbert's line.

He gave me a suspicious look when it was my turn, like he could tell by looking at me that I was out of place hob-knobbing with South Carolina's upper crust.

"You a friend of the family?"

"I'm a friend of the groom. We served together in the Army."

"What's your racket?"

"I'm a private investigator out of Baltimore. I should have said traveling salesman.

"You got a license?" It wasn't a friendly question.

"Do you need one to attend a wedding in this state?"

"No, so long as that's all you do. We don't take too kindly to private dicks poking their noses around in official investigations down in these parts."

"You don't have to worry about me. Murder isn't exactly my forte. I'm more of a missing person's type."

"Is that so? You look more the adultery type to me, chasing around cheating dames and lecherous husbands." At least he didn't say lost dogs.

"Adultery is an ugly word," I threw back.

"So is private investigator."

I almost pointed out that private investigator was actually two words but I thought better of it. The good sheriff and I were off to such a fine start I didn't want to rock the boat.

Chapter Eight

By the time I was finished with the police, Bradley, Lucy and Katherine were long gone. The only ones left were people I didn't know, so I moseyed back to my room and tried to get some sleep.

My juices were flowing pretty good and my leg was giving me a fit. I knew sleep wouldn't be part of my foreseeable future, so I pulled myself out of the sack and got dressed. I figured a belt of the hooch might do the trick and I made my way back downstairs to the bar. Some of the others had the same idea.

There was a seat open next to a little redhead who looked like she was working on a first rate drunk and I planted myself beside her. The bartender came over and I ordered my usual.

"Can I get you a drink?" I asked red.

"No thanks, I'm only having one." It must have been a pretty good one judging by the way she was teetering on her stool and slurring her words. She had an empty martini glass in front of her.

The girl looked to be in her mid-thirties and attractive in a wholesome, plain, and been around the block kind of way. Her hair was long and pulled back behind the ears and she was wearing a conservative grey dress suit. I couldn't tell if it was from drinking or crying but her eyes were red and maybe a little puffy.

There was a modest wedding ring on her finger.

She turned back toward me and stared for a moment like she was having trouble focusing in on me. "I know you," she finally said. "You're Bradley's army buddy, the flat foot from up north. I recognize you from the party."

"Not actually a flat foot but yes," I replied, holding out my hand to shake hers. "Frankie McKeller."

She looked at my hand for a second, bobbing a bit unsteady on her stool before turning back to her empty glass and trying unsuccessfully to extract another sip from it. "Dorothy White," she said as she sat it back down.

"You sure I can't get you another one, Dorothy?"

Dorothy shook her head no, staring forward at the bar back.

"Are you a friend of Bradley's?"

"Hardly, I work at the firm with Bradley and his father. I'm the secretary there."

"So you knew Tucker Morgan," I said, stating the obvious. "Sorry to hear about all that."

She took a deep breath like I'd hit a nerve and I could tell she was trying not to cry. "Yeah, I knew Tuck, all right. He was a good egg. It ain't fair the way he winded up."

I didn't say anything.

"Tuck was the best guy at that stupid company. Why, I got a mind to walk right in there on Monday morning and quit."

"You don't like working there?"

"What's to like? A bunch of back-stabbing money grubbers is all they are. They don't care nothing for nobody. You take Tuck, he was the most loyal, hard working guy in the place and you see the way the old man treated him."

"How's that?"

"Tuck practically ran that office before Bradley joined the firm. He should have been made a full partner, all the money he made for the firm. But how does old man Chilton repay him? He demotes him so his son can step in and take over. It just ain't fair."

"No, I guess in a way it's not."

"Heck, Tuck never complained. He went right on being loyal to the old man. Took on every dirty job they gave him.

Never complained, never missed a day's work, just went about his business.

"I know there were people who didn't like Tuck. Some thought he was just like the Chiltons but that was all business. He had another side to him. You think he liked doing some of the things he had to do? You bet he didn't, but he did what he had to because that's the kind of guy Tuck was. He was a good egg, that Tuck."

"That's what I hear."

"You're dang right," she slurred, fighting to keep her balance on the barstool. "Tuck was more loyal to the old man than his own son. Heck, those two are constantly going at it."

"I know Bradley has had some disagreements with his father."

"Disagreements? Bradley goes out of his way to spite his father. Why do you think he's getting married here? The old man wanted the wedding to be held at the family estate but Bradley wouldn't hear of it. He kept going on about how he loved the ocean and how it had to be here. This little wing ding is costing the old man a pretty penny, I can tell you that.

"I'll let you in on a little secret about Bradley Chilton. I shouldn't, seeing how you're his friend and all, but you ought to know. Bradley hates his father, literally hates the man. He'd do just about anything to one up the old skin flint."

"That seems a bit harsh," I added.

"You don't know harsh, the way he treats the old man. Sneaking around, going against his wishes, running the company any way he wants. Tuck wasn't like that at all. Maybe he didn't particularly like the old geezer but he respected him, respected his wishes. You see what that got him.

"I'll let you in on another thing about your friend Bradley. He's a momma's boy through and through, loves that woman more than anything. The way she ended up it's no wonder he hates the old man like he does. I guess she got it better than Tuck."

"You can't think that the Chiltons had anything to do with Tucker's death ... do you?"

Dorothy looked hard at me, swaying on her stool. "I don't think nothing. You could have done it for all I know. I'm just saying it wasn't right the way they treated ole Tuck. Besides, the

Chiltons wouldn't kill nobody, that's not their style. They have guys like Bowman to do their dirty work."

"Bowman?"

"I'm not saying Chet Bowman had anything to do with it either. I don't know from nothing. "

From there she went on about the Chiltons being crooked and greedy, repeating herself over and over. I chalked most of it up to the drunken ramblings of a grief stricken and disgruntled employee. There was no doubt in my mind that much of what she was saying was based in fact. After all, you don't get the kind of money the Chiltons have by playing nice all the time. I doubted if it went any deeper than that.

I was on my third whiskey and fifth cigarette when we were interrupted by a guy in pajamas and a very familiar looking Ocean Forest bathrobe. "Dottie, you got any idea what time it is?"

The guy was of average size and build with dark, coarse features, his salt and pepper hair tussled like he just woke up.

"I don't care what time it is, I'm just having a little drink."

"Who's this guy?" he asked, referring to me and not making any effort to be polite about it.

"He's a friend of Bradley's."

Her husband shot me a look. It was one of those threatening kind of looks that's meant to convey a message. "The lady is spoken for," he informed me.

"That's fine by me. I was just having a nightcap."

"Don't be like that, Charlie. We were just talking."

"Just talking, huh? Well the talking is over. It's time to come to bed." Charlie was still giving me the evil eye.

"I was thinking of having another drink."

"You're done drinking for the night."

I didn't much care for the husband but I figured it was none of my concern and I turned back to my drink. I knew enough to stay out of domestic quarrels.

"My friend died, Charlie, I want to have another."

Charlie let out a loud breath of disgust. "And good riddens to him, you're coming with me."

"Now, Charlie, that ain't no way to talk," she moaned.

"Dottie, do you really want to get into this right here?"

Dorothy thought about it for a moment before sliding her empty glass away and standing up. She went peacefully with him without any further argument.

The weird scene got me thinking. Things seemed to be adding up in that way they do when you have a couple of pieces of a puzzle and try to see the big picture.

The Charlie guy hadn't been a fan of Tucker Morgan; that was for certain. It was pretty obvious that his wife was, as she'd been pretty broken up by his death. Maybe it was nothing, a grieving coworker, a jealous husband. Like I said, it got me thinking. Thinking is an occupational hazard of my profession.

Chapter Nine

*I*t was quarter till five when I paid my tab and left the Brook-green Room. My leg was all but numb and the rest of me was feeling pretty good. I decided to take a walk back upstairs by the main entrance to check things out.

Sure enough, there was a deputy standing guard at the door. Standing might be a stretch. The guy was propped up on a stool and leaning against the wall. From where I stood, I couldn't even tell if he was awake. I'm guessing you could have snuck a herd of elephants out the door.

I took a little walk through the hotel, familiarizing myself with the surroundings, not quite ready to turn in. Past the lobby, across from the main entrance, was another set of doors that led out to a large veranda set with tables and chairs, guarded by another sleeping cop. Beyond that was a stone staircase which descended through a gothic looking arched overhang held up by stone pillars. The stairs bottomed out to the back lawn of the Ocean Forest, a long wide stretch where patrons could picnic and lounge, or partake in games of croquet and badminton.

From there you walked out beyond the hotel grounds and crossed over a small dirt road where a thin wooden walkway began and took you out further, eventually giving way to sand. I didn't have to hear the crashing waves or feel the thick salty breeze on my face to know where I was heading. I continued on, past the tall sea grass and sand dunes to where the world opened up into mind boggling vastness, and I stood staring out at the Atlantic Ocean.

She was wide and wondrous, stretching out as far as I could see. Gentle ripples skimmed along the top of her and the bright moonlight twinkled off her surface, a liquid carpet of constant motion that sprawled out across the dark horizon.

I felt a twinge in my gut and I thought of the last time I had seen her, of that horrific day when everything about me changed. There was a sharp pain in my leg but I knew it wasn't real; the whiskey had taken away the real thing. This pain pretended to be in my leg but it was more in my head, burned into my memory.

It was the pain of fear, of remembering something you tried to push out of your mind but knew it would always be a part of you. It was the pain of feeling your flesh give way and facing your own mortality, of knowing you were a goner and not being able to do anything about it.

This was the pain that no amount of booze could take away, the pain of seeing yourself honestly for the first time and thinking it would probably be the last. The pain I was feeling was the same pain I had felt on that beach two years before, the pain of looking at myself and realizing, for the first time, I was a coward.

I stood there for a long time, watching the waves roll in, feeling the sand give way under my feet, thinking, remembering. Memories washed over me, memories I hadn't thought of in ages. One of the things I remembered was why I hated the ocean.

I turned to leave and caught a glimpse of something up the beach. Off in the distance, there was another person out there, standing ankle deep in the waves, looking out over the Atlantic, like myself. The outline was visible but the details were lost in the darkness.

After staring awhile I began to think I could make them out. The long gown, dipped into the water, sticking to her wet body, the open robe whipping in the wind, the long hair blowing back with every gust. It looked a lot like Katherine Mathews. Maybe it was just my eyes playing tricks on me. Whoever it was, they looked like they wanted to be alone.

I turned and made my way back into the hotel.

As I got out of the elevator at my floor, I spotted a guy a few doors down, fumbling with a key, unsteady on his feet. The guy was wrecked, like he'd been on a major bender. He dropped his key to the floor and bent over to pick it up, almost falling over himself.

It was Gilbert Fleming. He was still trying to unlock his hotel room door when I let myself into my room and went off to bed. It was after six a.m.

Chapter Ten

*M*orning came way too soon. I woke up with the phone ringing. My head was pounding and my brain felt like it was drying out inside my skull. The thing inside my mouth felt something like my tongue but it tasted sour, seemed much too large and was covered in some sort of film. As far as hangovers go, it was a solid seven.

I reached out and grabbed the receiver. There was no wet in my throat and I tried to talk but couldn't squeeze out any sound.

"Frankie?" a voice asked. It was Bradley.

"Yeah," I managed in a cracking voice.

"Your presence is requested at breakfast."

"Breakfast?" I had heard of it but I just figured it was a rumor, something sober people came up with to screw with us drunks.

"Come on down, we're waiting on you."

"Call me back when lunch is served."

"Nonsense, you need to get down here. We've got eggs, bacon, sausage, pancakes, biscuits and gravy, and, of course, grits."

A queasy feeling settled into my gut. "I have no idea what grits might be but it sounds disgusting."

"You're going to love them, get down here."

"You got plain old coffee down there?"

"Come down and find out."

I glanced at my wrist watch, still on my arm. It was six forty-five.

Getting out of bed was torture. Putting my clothes on wasn't much better. Difficult as it was, I managed to get everything in the right place and head downstairs. The freckled faced kid was at the controls of the elevator again, he was giving me that look. The ride down seemed longer than before, and I decided to make small talk.

"You hear about what happened last night?"

"Yeah, everybody's heard."

"You were still working when it happened, weren't you?"

"I was here. I've been here all night. "

"Did you see anybody go up just before, anybody who looked like they might be kind of angry?"

"I saw a lot of people go up before. You were one of them."

"How about going down? You see anybody that maybe looked out of sorts?"

The kid looked me in the face and smiled. "I sure didn't see anybody that looked as out of sorts as you do now."

I was liking Freckle Face less and less.

On the back veranda, a place the locals referred to as Peacock Alley, most of the wedding party was already starting their day, scattered about the various tables. I spotted Bradley across the way. He was sitting with his parents, Lucy and Katherine.

The men were wearing, I later found out, golf attire, light pull-over sleeveless sweaters over collared shirts with three-quarter length pants and long patterned socks that were exposed up to the knee.

Bradley's mother was wearing a thin maroon dress with lots of ruffles and folds and an over-sized bonnet. She sat in front of a plate of food, staring off into the distance.

Lucy and Katherine were both wearing swim suits, Lucy's under an open cotton robe. If you haven't seen a swim suit lately, I can tell you they are nothing like the conservative bathing attire of years gone by.

Both were similar in style, strapless and leaving the shoulders exposed, leading down to low cut fronts that all but revealed the very tops of their chests — Katherine's nearly busting out — and hugging the sides of their torsos. From there they tapered revealingly down the body, the fabric stretching across the contours of their curves, leaving little to the imagination. There were no bloomers to speak of with the one piece suits and they simply ended at the very tops of the girl's thighs, tucking in snug about their bottoms, and leaving the whole of their long legs for everyone to see, Lucy's toned and tanned, Katherine's a soft delicate mix of milk white and pink that seemed to go on forever. Lucy's suit was red; Katherine's a light shade of blue. Before the war, an outfit as such would have turned more than a few heads. Living in the modern world certainly had its advantages and even in my tattered state I got a little thrill out of sitting down with a couple of Pinup Models.

Lucy was wearing a large floppy hat, straw with a red ribbon hanging from it. Katherine's head was bare, her blonde hair hanging long and haphazard over her shoulders, unruly and free. Everyone at the table was wearing shaded glasses.

I took the empty seat beside Katherine and tried not to stare at her exposed legs. "Good morning," I said.

"Lord, Frankie, you're going to suffocate in those clothes," Bradley pointed out. I was wearing a grey wool suit. "We're going to have to find you something more suitable to wear."

Disregarding the remark, I took the over turned coffee cup from in front of me and filled it from the pot in the center of the table. Nursing the precious cup in both hands, I took three large gulps, ignoring the burning on my tongue and the scalding in my throat.

I sat contently waiting for the caffeine to kick in, feeling the morning elixir run down my insides, leaving a path of warmth in its wake. When I happened to look up, I realized that the entire table was staring at me, even Mrs. Chilton.

"What?"

Katherine laughed out loud. "Rough night?"

"What, can't a guy enjoy his morning coffee?"

They all joined in the laughter.

"If your eyes were any redder," she added, "we'd have to bandage them."

"I'm not much of a morning person."

"Eat up," the elder Chilton said. "We can't be lolly-gagging around here all morning."

"We have a golf date," Bradley added.

"No thanks. I'm not really a golfer."

"Nonsense, everyone plays golf." I guess in old man Chilton's world they probably did. "We have a tee time of seven thirty."

Great, I thought, now not only did I have to eat breakfast and play golf, I have to attend some kind of early morning tea party too. It was later explained to me what a tee time was.

I picked at a piece of sausage and some scrambled eggs, draining two more cups of coffee, the later one I even managed to sneak a shot of booze into. Before long I was feeling human again.

"What are you girls going to do while we're out golfing?" I asked Katherine but Lucy answered.

"Bradley suggested the two of us take a dip in the ocean." She sounded as if she were making sure everyone knew it wasn't her idea.

"Yes," Katharine agreed, "it should be loads of fun." Neither woman sounded too thrilled with the prospect.

"Why don't you two play a spot of tennis while we're out?" Bradley said, then looking at me, "Lucy is quite the athlete."

His fiancé shot him one of those looks a girl shoots her man when he sticks his foot in his mouth then turned to Katherine with a forced smile. "I don't think I'm feeling up for tennis. I'm afraid I may have twisted my ankle." It seemed a pretty lame excuse to get out of tennis with her fiancé's ex.

"I don't think I'm up for tennis either," Katherine agreed. You got the sense that the two weren't too high on the idea of spending a lot of alone time together.

"Well, I'm sure you girls will find something to keep yourself occupied," the old man inserted. "Maybe we can all meet back here for a late lunch."

I'd been around this lot long enough to know they were some strange birds, consumed with keeping up appearances, as Katherine had put it, but I was struck by the state of denial they seemed to be in. No one acted like somebody they all knew had taken a bullet to the brain the night before. I thought maybe it was time to stir a little reality into the stew.

"What about Sheriff Talbert? Didn't he say he wanted to question everyone this morning?"

"Hogwash," the old man quipped. "There'll be plenty of time for that later. Besides, it's not like anyone at this table had anything to do with it."

"No, but someone among us might possess valuable information that could aid in the investigation."

"I find that highly unlikely. None of us would consort with the kind of person capable of such a deed."

"I quite agree," Bradley added. "My guess is it was the work of some common thief, an act of burglary."

"Was anything taken?"

Bradley smiled. "I don't know, but it wouldn't be uncommon for Tucker to be carrying large sums of cash. He was frequently working on various land deals for the firm. Isn't that right, Father?"

The old man looked lost for a second but regained his composure. "Quite right, in fact there was some kind of deal he wanted to talk to me about last night. He seemed rather adamant about it."

"It kind of makes you wish you'd taken the time to hear him out," I added.

"I'll have Dorothy run down to the office and check the safe, see if any petty cash is missing."

I looked over to Lucy. "Have you talked to your brother this morning?"

She smiled. "Why, yes, I have. In fact, I talked to him last night as well. Immediately after I talked to the sheriff I went directly to his room."

"And he was there?" I asked, knowing full well he wasn't.

"Yes, he'd been there all evening, I woke him up, actually. The poor soul was so distraught over poor Tucker's death that I ended up sitting up and consoling him for most of the night. He was really very fond of Tucker."

Bradley took her hand. "Poor chap, it's a tough break."

Katherine fidgeted in her chair and took a sip of coffee; she seemed to be purposely not looking toward the happy couple. Suddenly she stood up and excused herself, citing the fact that she may have had a bit too much to drink the night before. I guess that one mint julep she nursed was stronger than I thought.

You don't have to drive a meat truck to know a load of baloney when you see it. I chalked it up to the keeping up of appearances thing. They weren't the kind of people who wanted to be pulled into a nasty scandal.

"Good morning, folks," Sheriff Talbert said as he approached our table. He looked about as bad as I felt. I could only imagine he'd been up all night working on the case.

"Good morning, Sheriff," the old man said for all of us.

"I wonder if I might have a word with you folks." Talbert's words were cautious and courteous.

"Actually, we have plans for the morning. Would you mind if we were to postpone it until this afternoon, maybe after lunch?" Mr. Chilton asked as if he were acquiring about the time.

The sheriff's face turned three shades of red. "After lunch? What's the hurry, a man has only been murdered? Maybe we could get together some time next week and discuss it over a game of croquet."

"Listen here, Sheriff, we're all perfectly willing to cooperate — "

Talbert cut him off. "Yeah, that's what I keep hearing."

"It's just that we have a fairly busy weekend planned."

"Is that so? I hear Tucker Morgan had a pretty busy weekend planned too."

Old man Chilton cleared his throat, as he was prone to do in awkward situations. "I suppose we could postpone our plans for a bit if it would help."

"Gee, that would be peachy of you," Talbert said, pulling up a chair and wedging it in between Mr. and Mrs. Chilton. He pointed to the coffee mug in front of Mrs. Chilton, still overturned. "You using that?"

Mrs. Chilton looked at him like he was speaking Japanese.

"Help yourself," her husband answered for her.

The sheriff took the cup and began filling it from the pot, still looking at Mrs. Chilton. "So, where were you during all the excitement last night?"

Now she was looking at him like he was diseased.

"My wife was with me, in our room."

"She doesn't speak?"

The throat clearing. "My wife suffers from a condition … "

"Ok," Talbert said, turning to Chilton, "so the two of you were tucked in all nice and cozy for the night?"

"We had retired for the evening."

Sheriff Talbert turned his attention to Bradley and Lucy, taking a long drink from his cup. "You the ones getting hitched?" he asked.

"Yes, they are the wedding couple," the old man answered.

"Anybody, besides Mr. Chilton here, capable of speaking?"

"Lucy and I had gone to bed as well," Bradley replied.

"In separate rooms?"

"See here, Sheriff," the old man blurted out.

"No, it's all right, Father. As a matter of fact, we were in separate rooms. I had walked Lucy to her room where we said our goodnights, and then I went back to my room. I had just gotten there when I heard the shot."

"Anybody see you?"

"I don't know."

"What floor are you staying on?"

"Lucy's on the fourth floor; I'm on the third."

"The same as Tucker. You must have been on the scene pretty quick, considering you hadn't actually gone to bed yet."

"I suppose I got there rather quickly."

"And you didn't see anything out of the ordinary?"

"I'd say everything I saw was rather out of the ordinary. It's not like this kind of thing happens to us very often."

Katherine was just returning to the table and Sheriff Talbert turned to her. "What floor are you staying on?"

"I'm on the fourth floor, next to Lucy."

"Where were you when the shot went off?"

"I was in bed; it woke me from a sound sleep," she informed him. "By the time I got there a crowd had gathered outside the room. I'm afraid I couldn't be of much help either."

"You were alone?"

Katherine blushed a little and shifted in her seat. "Yes, Sheriff, I was quite alone."

65

"How about you?" It was my turn.

"I'm on the third floor, a few doors down from Morgan. I was alone in bed. When I heard the shot I threw on a robe and rushed out to see what all the hoopla was. There were a few people in the hall when I got there, nobody I recognized and nobody who looked like they had just offed anyone."

"Does anyone have anything to add?"

I thought twice about bringing it up for Lucy's sake but spit it out anyway. "Earlier in the evening, as I was going back to my room I saw Tucker outside his door with Gilbert Fleming. They appeared to be in a heated debate."

Lucy shot me a look that could melt ice.

Talbert scrolled through a note pad. "Gilbert Fleming, this is the same guy Morgan got into it with at the party?"

"I wouldn't say got into it," Lucy chimed in.

"What would you say?"

"I would say the two had words."

"There are those at the party who say he seemed pretty agitated with Morgan."

"The two were old and dear friends," Lucy explained. "Friends tend to argue at times. It was nothing."

"He is your brother, isn't he?"

"Yes, he is."

The sheriff turned back to me. "How heated would you say this debate they were having was?"

"It didn't look like anybody was going to plug anybody over it, if that's what you mean."

"How well did you know the deceased?" Still at me.

"I met him last night for about a minute."

"And Gilbert Fleming?"

"The same."

He went around the table for the next twenty minutes, grilling us on this and that, a rapid fire assault of questions. Never once did he seem pleased or displeased with any of our answers.

Talbert made some notes in his pad before standing up. "I'll tell you what, I don't want a little thing like a homicide to screw up y'alls weekend. You're free to go about your business for now but I'm going to need to speak to each of you again later today, if that's all right with you, Mr. Chilton."

"Of course, whatever you need, Sheriff."

Sheriff Talbert made his way to the next table, and the rest of us sat in silence for a few moments, no one knowing what to say. Then the old man took charge in his usual way.

"Well, then, if we hurry we can still make that tee time."

Chapter Eleven

*B*radley offered to lend me a pair of knickers but I politely declined. I'm not really the *knicker* type.

They had the car brought around and they whisked me out the front door. The car wasn't anything like the sort of jalopies I was used to riding in. It was a pre-war Cadillac convertible but it looked brand new, long and lean, white and immaculate.

Bradley drove with his father in the passenger seat and me tucked in behind them. As we were pulling away from the Ocean Forest, I sat back in the seat and took a long look at the old gal.

They called her The Million Dollar Hotel and for good reason. Even seventeen years after going up she looked worth every penny of it. She was gigantic, housing two hundred and two rooms, half facing the Atlantic and the other half facing the forest across the street. Her face was white stone with a copper roof and she stretched out long across the front, four floors running the length of her. In the center a tall tower shot up into the sky like a temple, three windows wide and extending her another six stories. There were another two columns protruding at the sides of the tower and jutting out forward, housing additional rooms in each, huge luxurious rooms from the looks of it.

She was as grand and majestic as anything I had ever seen. Her back drop was the blue South Carolina sky and the Atlantic

Ocean. Staring up at her was like looking at a postcard of a place you could never hope to visit.

We pulled out past the main driveway and down the street, toward something the old man called the Ocean Forest Club. It had been called that at one time. Bradley drove slow and easy like he had nowhere in particular to be, down Calhoun Road, past the odd octagonal building which housed much of the Ocean Forest staff that the locals called the bullpen. Farther down, across the main drag, with the gentle rolling greens of the Pine Lakes Country Club to our left, we came to the club's main building, regal and Southern like Tara in *Gone with the Wind*, a simple little number that housed sixty-four rooms. At one time the Ocean Forest Club boasted twenty-two tennis courts, two golf courses, horse stables and riding trails along with an array of other sporting opportunities built into the forest surrounding it. These Southerners certainly knew how to occupy their free time.

By now, Pine Lakes had branched off into its own country club, its course the oldest in the area. Most everyone around simply referred to it as the Grandaddy. The course looked like something cut from heaven, her long green fairways as cool and smooth as the surface of the freshwater lakes along the course. The grass was trimmed to perfection and the most vibrant green I had ever seen and it seemed a crime to allow people to walk on it. They didn't have such places in Baltimore City or if they did, they hid them pretty well.

I'm not sure I would have been a particularly good golfer before my leg got busted up but after I had no chance at all. Bradley and the old man kept trying to give me pointers, keep your back straight, follow through with your swing. The more advice they gave me, the shoddier I seemed to get.

All things considered, I had a pretty good time and I realized early on that the only way to truly enjoy the game was not to worry about your score. There are worse ways to spend a morning. We spent the next four hours chasing a little white ball around the quiet lush greens of the Pine Lakes Golf Course.

Old man Chilton kept talking about how much he loved the game but you'd never know it by the way he cussed and carried on after almost every shot he took. He was a piece of work, the old bird.

Halfway through the back nine, Bradley was setting up for his next shot. He was a hundred and fifty yards away from the green and off to the right of the fairway with a cluster of small trees about twenty-five yards in front of him. He asked his caddy for a seven iron.

"A seven iron?" the old man asked with a huff. "You'll never clear those trees with a seven iron. Go with the nine iron."

"I can reach the green with the seven iron."

"Not if you hit those trees. You're going to need more loft, go with the nine."

"I can do it."

"Nonsense, don't be stupid, play it safe and go with the nine."

"With all due respect, Father, I know what I'm doing here. The seven iron, please."

The caddy handed him the seven iron. Bradley spent an inordinate amount of time setting himself up, eyeing the distance and figuring the trajectory of his shot. His concentration was intense, his form impeccable, his swing perfection. He hit the tree like he was aiming for it.

"I told you to go with the nine iron."

I got the feeling the argument didn't have much to do with golf clubs and it wasn't the first time they'd had it.

As we were walking up the course, I tried to lighten up the tension between the two of them. "This is quite the town you have here."

"We like it. Of course, we don't actually live here. Nobody lives in Myrtle Beach, we summer here. Most of us live in Charleston but we do keep an office here. Father also owns a Farm Supply store in town."

"Locals?" I asked.

"Some but it gets pretty quiet in the off-season."

"The town started as a timber colony," old man Chilton informed me. "It wasn't incorporated until thirty-eight."

"This place is a goldmine," Bradley added. "It could be the tourist Mecca of the east coast one day."

"Hogwash," his father snorted. "Tourism won't fly here.

They tried back in twenty-six but it didn't take off. They opened the Ocean Forest in twenty-nine, thinking this was going to be the next vacation capital of the Eastern Seaboard. The plan was to build an all inclusive resort for members only called Arcady. It was going to be the ultimate playground for the wealthy and privileged but you see how that turned out. The very course we're playing started off as part of that ill-fated experiment.

"There will always be people who will come here because it's secluded and personal and because of the pristine beaches but the future of Myrtle Beach is in agriculture and industry. That's how this town is going to grow."

"Father, the potential of Myrtle Beach in tourism is astronomical, as I keep telling you."

Chilton turned to me. "My son is stubborn, he refuses to see things the way they are. He chooses to ignore the lessons history has taught us."

"It was during the Great Depression," Bradley argued. "How many people were vacationing?"

"Bradley is a bit short sighted when it comes to seeing the world in realistic terms."

"I'm the short sighted one?"

"Take your bride to be, for example."

"Don't let's get started with that again."

"Lucy is a lovely girl but let's not fool ourselves. Do you think that Herbert Fleming isn't salivating at the prospect of getting his hands in my pockets?" The old man was coarse and blunt.

"It isn't all about you and your money."

"Please, the Flemings don't have a proverbial pot."

It was about as salty as I had heard the old man get, discounting the aftermath of a few of his golf shots.

"The Flemings happen to own quite a bit of land in the area."

"Salt marsh, practically worthless."

"Salt marsh?" I asked. "I thought they owned a bunch of swamp land."

"No," Bradley corrected me. "Salt marsh is a whole different animal. Salt marsh is nothing like swamp, it can easily be made usable."

"At great expense," his father added.

"Expensive, yes, but if that land were utilized to its full potential, the investment would be well worth it."

"Such as tourism, I suppose."

"Exactly, as I've told you a thousand times."

"Ludicrous."

Bradley shook his head.

"Your choices in life have been less than stellar. It could be worse, though. You could have married Katherine Mathews."

"Don't you dare speak ill of Katherine." Bradley shot back and his face was flushed with anger. "Katherine is a wonderful woman."

"So she is," Chilton replied, calm and cool, "but she isn't much better off than the Flemings."

"You think that just because people don't have as much as you they're not as good as you."

The old man stopped walking and turned back to his son. "You're a dreamer, Bradley. You fail to see the world as it really is."

"I see the world as it could be," Bradley corrected his father. The two stood looking at each other for a few moments, both looking at the other but neither seeing past the impression of each in their own minds. I couldn't help but feel sorry for the two of them and I wasn't even sure why.

Clouds had been rolling in for awhile, a storm heading in off the ocean. All at once, it broke loose in a down pour like I had never witnessed. Rain was coming down in buckets, drenching us to the bone and making it impossible to continue with our game. We rushed off to the clubhouse, that intimate sixty four room manor, where we had cocktails and sat drying out.

The arguments between Bradley and his father continued, rehashing the same old ground. It was painful to watch.

Eventually, the storm passed and the sun came back out. Still soaking wet, we made our way back to the car and drove back through the largely undeveloped area that should have been Arcady to the Ocean Forest Hotel.

Chapter Twelve

By the time we got back to the hotel the storm had passed and it was sunny and hot again. Mr. Chilton went off to his room to change; I went with Bradley to his. It was two doors down from the one where Tucker Morgan was murdered.

Bradley gave me a bathing suit to change into. I was dead set against the idea, not being the swimsuit type but Bradley insisted. After I put it on I felt ridiculous in the baggy shorts with my bare chest exposed and elected to wear a sleeveless undershirt with them.

"You look good," he lied.

"I look like a dolt."

"Do I look like a dolt?" He was wearing an almost identical suit, sans the shirt. He did not look like a dolt. He was tall and muscular, tanned, trim and athletic. He looked like he belonged in the suit.

Me, on the other hand, I looked weak and scrawny, pale and sickly. To make matters worse, all I could think about was the huge scar that started at the back of my right thigh and circled around my leg, extending down to the center of my calf. It was hideous and gruesome and I had never been out in public with it exposed.

"You're being silly," he assured me. "No one is going to notice."

We made our way downstairs and out the back of the hotel. Lucy and Katherine were sitting at the same table they had been earlier. To my delight, they were still wearing their swimsuits.

"Look at you," Katherine said as we approached. "You're looking quite debonair in that bathing suit." I knew she was lying.

"Bradley made me wear it."

"I like it."

"Who's up for a swim?" Bradley asked.

"Not me," I answered.

"What's the matter, McKeller, can't swim?" Katherine asked in a flirty tone.

"It's Frankie, actually, and as a matter of fact..."

"Not to worry, I'll be close by in case you start to drown, Frankie."

On a scale of one ten, ten being the thing I least wanted to do, swimming in the ocean would have rated a fifty-eight but there was a part of me that liked the idea of being with Katherine even in the water.

She looked gorgeous in her skimpy little swimsuit, every curve of her body pressed tight against the thin material. Her skin was pinkish and smooth, a healthy glow radiating about her. Her face was devoid of any makeup and a little more plain than it had been the night before, but it made her look softer and more lovely than I remembered her. Those big brown eyes seemed to light up in the sunshine, the whites around them brighter than any I had ever seen. At that moment, she could have talked me into just about anything.

"OK."

"Up," she ordered. I complied. Katherine took out a jar of some concoction that smelled of cocoanut. She scooped some out and began applying it to my arms, shoulders and face. It went on greasy and felt strange, but I liked the feel of her soft hands rubbing it into my skin.

"Lubing me up?" I asked.

"Sunburn ointment, it helps prevent burning." I could have stood there all day.

The four of us grabbed beach towels from the cabana boy

and headed off, across the dirt road and down the planked walk-way toward the surf. The sun was blinding and coarse, bathing the scene in intense light, making everything look like a color snapshot. The sky was bluer than I'd ever seen, the ocean an emerald green, alive and mammoth.

I was a bit more hesitant than the rest as they went running out into the waves.

They rushed in, diving into the water, submerging them-selves in the surf and basking in the sunshine. Playing, yelling and splashing each other, they took to it like they had been doing it all their lives. They had.

I eased myself into the water, taking small careful steps, inching my way into the dreaded Atlantic. The sand seemed to move under my feet and the waves kept pushing me back while the undercurrent tried to pull me out. I felt off balance and awk-ward as I stepped deeper into her bosom.

This was something that I had promised myself I would never do again, yet here I was. It had been just over two years since I had last set foot in her.

Not that this was much like the last time. Before, she had been cold and unyielding, horrific and judgmental, daring me to confront her.

Now she was warm, like bath water, light and whimsical, inviting me to lose myself in her body, to let go of the fears I harbored of her. If only it was that easy.

Part of me loved the way she soothed my skin against the harsh South Carolina heat, enveloping me in the brisk coolness of her waves, devouring me in the comfort of her. Another part could feel the sheer power of her, the divine emptiness of her depths, the living breathing entity that she was, the force I was no match for.

She toyed with me, slapping at my shins, daring me to go deeper. I couldn't. I froze in place, sweat running down my face, my body rigid with fear.

Memories I had pushed out of my brain came flooding back, explosions, gunfire, the salty copper mix of blood and saltwater in my mouth. My brain cramped and I couldn't breathe. Pain shot up my leg and I was living that day all over again.

I heard the screams of men, the smell of fresh gunpowder in the air and the sky grew dark and grey. My body began to tremble and I looked down to my feet. I was knee deep in the water.

"Frankie, are you OK?" Bradley asked. The others had stopped what they were doing, all three staring back at me like I was some sort of freak.

I couldn't answer. My body was like cement and my mind was spinning with a million thoughts, my voice a forgotten vehicle I no longer knew how to control.

Katherine waded over to me, taking me by the arm. Her touch was warm and comforting, all of me wanting to collapse into her. She pulled at me, turning me back and walking me out of the surf.

She took me to a spot on the beach where she spread a couple of towels and helped me lower myself onto one. She sat down next to me. Lucy and Bradley were asking us if everything were all right. Katherine assured them it was.

While they went back to playing in the water, Katherine leaned herself in next to me, pressing herself into my side, letting me know she was there. "Is everything OK?" she asked.

"Yeah, I'm fine."

"You don't look fine."

My breathing was returning to normal and I could feel my body relaxing. "I'm OK. I just don't like the ocean much."

"Does it have something to do with that scar on your leg?"

Instinctively, my hand reached down and tried in vain to cover it. She placed her hand over mine and pulled it away, exposing my scar. Then she did something that no human being had ever done. She laid her hand over the area, touching it gently with her fingertips.

"How did it happen?"

"The war," I answered.

"I figured that much."

I shrugged. "It was Omaha Beach, I caught some shrapnel."

"Lucy says Bradley saved your life in the war. He never talks about it."

"That's the truth, he did. He's a regular hero."

"What about you? You were wounded in battle, you're a

hero too. "

"No, I'm really not."

She smiled and tilted her head into me, resting it on my shoulder. "You're being modest."

I felt something churning in my gut. Maybe it was her skin on my arm, her warmth seeping in with mine. Maybe it was the dark secret within me, bubbling about, daring me to let it out. Whatever it was, I was overcome with the urge to share something with this person I had never shared with anyone else. It would be the first time I had ever heard the story said aloud.

"Bradley and I had been serving together almost two years by that point. We'd been through a lot and we were waiting on D-Day."

Katherine shifted her face slightly, pressing herself into me more. There was no turning back.

"We had been on that bucket for over a week, waiting to get the go for the invasion. I was sea sick the whole time, a real mess. I couldn't wait to get off that boat.

"I wasn't sure what had happened when the shell went off. Everything went blurry and I felt this sharp pain in my leg like it was being ripped in half. Explosions are a weird thing; it's like the air turns to steel and slams into you with the force of a Mack truck. You can't breath, you can't think, you're brains get jumbled around.

"I remember being thrown from the craft, the feeling of falling, hitting the water. At this point, I was still conscious somehow, and I remember sinking into the sea, the taste of salt in my mouth, burning in my eyes, the coldness surrounding me. The ocean was swallowing me up and there was nothing I could do about it.

"I was aware of what was happening and I knew that I was going to die. My arms and legs wouldn't respond to my brain. There was a voice in my head that kept screaming, 'Swim you stupid bastard, swim!' but I couldn't. I just lay limp in the water.

"Bradley had gotten off the landing craft ahead of me, and I guess he looked back just in time to see the shell hit. He came back for me. I had given up and was just taking in a gulp of seawater, unable to hold my breath any longer."

At this point Lucy and Bradley were wrestling in the water, frolicking and laughing, indifferent to Katherine and me on the beach.

"I felt a tug at my collar and something lifted me into the air, someone pulling me along, holding me above the waves.

"When we hit the beach it was complete and utter chaos. Bradley was on his hands and knees, dragging me behind him, pulling me over the bodies and debris that littered the surf. The noise was like nothing you could imagine, gun shots, artillery, men screaming and crying for help.

"Bradley was yanking me up the sand a few feet at a time and I was puking blood and saltwater, dead weight, offering no help at all. At some point, he was down at my leg wrapping some sort of bandage around it. I remember screaming bloody murder, begging him to stop.

"The shock was wearing off and the pain was unbearable. I tried to sit up, and I caught a glimpse of my wound, my fatigues shredded and the meat of my leg sticking out the back and side.

"Bradley's hands were covered in my blood. I yelled at him to leave me, to stop hurting me, but he told me shut the hell up. He told me I was going with him and I had no say in it."

Katherine lifted her head, turning to look out at Bradley, playing in the water with Lucy, maybe imagining him on that day.

"Once he got the bleeding under control, he wrapped my arm around his shoulder and stood us up. 'Run, Frankie,' he told me and I tried, but I didn't have much in the tank. He carried me up to the dunes and dropped me in behind them.

"He carried me with him all day, nursing my leg, taking care of me. Eventually, after things had settled down, he got me to an aid station. He saved my life, pure and simple."

"That's why you hate the water?" she asked, stating the obvious.

"That's why I hate the ocean."

"What Bradley did that day was certainly heroic, but you were there too. What you did was heroic as well."

"No." I shook my head.

I looked into her deep brown eyes, and I felt an intense connection to this woman I had only known for a day or so.

There was something in those eyes that made me feel safe and at ease; it made me want to cleanse my soul and open up completely to her. When I went to speak again my voice trembled and stalled. The words caught in the back of my throat, but I swallowed hard and forced them out, determined to complete my confession.

"I turned back when the ramp dropped," I said.

Katherine looked puzzled.

"When we were about to deploy, they lowered the ramp on the landing craft and the bullets were flying ... bodies bobbing in the surf ...

"The world was a thundering mix of confusion and insanity, fallen and broken men as far as you could see. I looked out at the carnage in front of me and I panicked. My first instinct was to turn and run but there was nowhere to go. I turned and tried to go back, fighting against the other men trying to get out of the landing craft. That's what I was doing when the shell went off.

"Who knows how many of those guys didn't get off that boat because they had to get through me."

There was a long pause. In my mind I was cursing myself, regretting telling her my darkest secret, wishing I could take it back. Hearing it aloud made it seem even more wretched than I had imagined it in the dark recesses of my mind.

It was then that Katherine did something astounding. She reached up, placing her hand on my cheek and pulled me toward her. She pulled me in until our faces were touching and she kissed me long and softly on the lips.

That kiss was unlike anything I had ever experienced, before or since. Her lips were warm and delicate and I felt it through my entire body. Even my self-loathing seemed to slip away, if only for a moment.

Katherine backed away slightly, our faces still close together. "You had been sick for a week. You weren't in your right mind. You weren't thinking straight. Anybody could have reacted the same way. "

"Anybody didn't, I did."

"You were over there two years before that. What about the rest of the war? Does that one moment cancel out everything else you did over there?"

"Yes."

"It doesn't mean anything, stop beating yourself up over it."

"What are you two doing?" Bradley asked in a harsh voice, standing in front of us, dripping with water. Lucy was standing off behind him, still in the waves, looking on with confusion.

Katherine looked up at him and then back at Lucy. "What are you two doing?" She matched his angry tone.

"I'm having a swim with my fiancé."

"I'm talking with Frankie."

"Talking?"

"It's really none of your concern, Bradley."

"Well, I just thought …"

"Why don't you go back to your fiancé?"

Bradley stood there for awhile, unable to think of a decent reply. Lucy called for him to return to the water. He glanced back at her and then to us.

"Lucy is calling you," Katherine pointed out. "You should get back out there."

Reluctantly, Bradley made his way back out into the ocean.

That was the moment I knew for sure. That was the moment I knew Bradley was still very much in love with Katherine Mathews. I suspected, despite what I wanted to believe, that she was still in love with him as well.

Chapter Thirteen

*I*t felt good to be out of the silly swimsuit and back in grown up clothes. After spending an hour and a half on the beach with Katherine, I had gone up to my room for a quick bath and a change of clothes, back into my usual grey suit. The others were going up to their rooms for an afternoon nap. I considered doing the same but I'd had such little sleep I was afraid if I were to lie down I might sleep through the weekend.

The sunburn ointment worked fairly well and most of me felt pretty good but there were spots on my neck and back she had missed. I could feel the stinging singe of the burn setting in and I got the feeling it was going to get worse before it got better.

As I stepped out into the hallway, I glanced in the direction of Bradley's room just in time to see the door swing open. I jumped back into my own doorway, out of sight, a reflex action from the long hours I'd spent hiding in alleys and tailing cheating couples. Peeking back around, I spotted Katherine coming out of the room, Bradley behind her.

She stopped and turned back to him, leaning forward like she was going to give him a peck on the lips. Bradley backed away and she stopped herself, turning away and heading down the corridor, her back to me, her head hanging low.

I waited for a moment, giving time for Bradley to go back

81

into his room and Katherine to disappear around the corner. Then I left, fighting the jealous tension in my gut and headed for the elevator.

Freckled Face was at his usual position. He gave me the cold shoulder as we descended to the lobby. It was just as well, I wasn't in the mood for chit chat. My mind was busy slapping me in the face, asking myself what the hell I was mixed up in.

What was with Katherine and Bradley, Katherine and me? What was going on with all the lies and cover ups and half truths floating around? Why did it seem that everyone was trying to hide something? How did it all fit and did any of it have anything to do with the death of Tucker Morgan?

Maybe it was the detective in me but I found myself wanting answers. One thing I learned at the Staley School of Private Investigation is the quickest way to start getting answers is to start asking questions.

The lobby was sparse, most of the guests off doing beach things or back in their rooms resting. I looked around for a familiar face and spotted one sitting on a sofa across the way. It was Dorothy White and it seemed as good a place to start as any.

"Hello, Mrs. White, how are you today."

She was reading a dime store romance novel and didn't seem to hear me. "Mrs. White?" I tried again, "Dorothy?"

"White?" she asked, looking up from her book. "Nobody's called me that in awhile. My married name is Jackson."

"Sorry, my mistake."

She was in much better shape than the last time I had seen her, primped and fluffed, everything in place. The pale complexion in her cheeks was the only thing that gave a clue that she might be recovering from a grade-A hangover.

Dorothy looked at me strange, like she was trying to place me, unsure who I was. "Do I know you?"

"Frank McKeller, Bradley's friend."

She smiled up at me. "It's very nice to meet you."

"We actually met last night at the bar."

The color returned to her face and then some. "I'm afraid I had a bit much to drink last night. I don't remember much of anything."

"It's understandable, what with Tucker and all."

Her smile faded quick and there was a sadness in her eyes. "Yes, of course, it was a terrible tragedy." I sensed that she was holding back, trying to conceal the extent of her pain.

"He was a good egg," I added.

Tears welled up in her eyes and she blinked hard a few times, forcing the smile back on her face. "That he was."

"I was just wondering; I talked to Mr. Chilton earlier today and he said that Tucker might have been carrying a large sum of cash on him, something to do with a real estate deal he was working on. He said he was going to ask you to run to the office and check the petty cash and see if any was missing."

Dorothy shook her head slowly from side to side. "I don't know anything about it. He never mentioned anything to me."

"Do you know of any deals he might have been working on?"

"Tuck was always working on something but I doubt if he would have brought it here with him. The whole company is closed for the weekend, everyone's at the wedding. I can't imagine what it might have been."

"Isn't it strange to use cash in such things? I would think a cashier's check would be the way to go."

"Usually," she explained, "but it's not all that uncommon. There are some very old fashioned people in these parts, some of them are very leery of trusting checks and banks and such."

"I was just curious," I replied. "I'll let you get back to your book."

She held it up for me to see. "Trashy romance novels are my weakness."

"I'm more a detective story guy myself, the trashier the better."

We said our polite goodbyes and I asked her to say hello to Charlie for me.

"You know Charlie?"

"Oh yeah, Charlie and I go way back."

From there I headed downstairs to the bar, as I'm in the habit of doing. I figured a belt would clear my mind and help me think. I was surprised to find old man Chilton there, smoking a cigar and sipping on a snifter of brandy. He was sitting next to a guy in a black suit.

The guy was tall and husky with wide shoulders, a bit ominous looking and there was no drink in front of him. His face was long and pock marked. Dark eyes lingered under a thick black hairline that came half way down his forehead and his skin was the color of polished wood, like he spent most of his days in the sun.

As I approached, the guy stood up and put on his hat. He gave Chilton a nod and walked off, scorching me with a look as we passed each other.

"Good afternoon," Chilton greeted me.

"Afternoon," I responded, settling into the stool next to him and ordering a whiskey.

"You're just the fellow I wanted to speak with."

"Then this is your lucky day."

"You did a nice job out on the course today, not bad for a first timer."

"Thanks, is that what you wanted to talk to me about?"

"You're a right to the point kind of guy, I like that," he said with a sly smile.

"I find that beating around the bush usually just ends up screwing up the landscaping."

"Bradley tells me you're some kind of private investigator."

"Some kind."

"What if I were to hire you?" Now things were getting interesting.

"For what?"

"Let's say I wanted someone looking out for my interests in this matter, someone to look out for the interests of my people."

"As in?"

"As in making sure none of mine are implicated in this ugly state of affairs."

"Don't you mean that you want someone to find out who killed your long time employee?"

The old man took a sip from his snifter; I took a swig from my shot glass.

"The police will take care of that. I want someone to make sure no one in my circle gets dragged down into this dreadful situation."

"What if it turns out they are involved in this dreadful situation?"

"Impossible," he grunted.

"What if?"

The old man reached into his breast pocket and pulled out an envelope. It was your standard size business envelope and it had his company logo stenciled in the left hand corner. He placed it on the bar in front of me. "We'll deal with that when we get to it."

I picked up the envelope and opened it. It was stuffed with hundred dollar bills, crisp and new. I could almost smell the ink drying. There looked to be about three month's wages for me, three good months.

"I trust that should suffice as a suitable retainer."

Pulling a half empty pack of Lucky Strikes from my pocket, I slid one out and lit it. Sitting back in my stool, I stared back at the old geezer.

He had an aura of power about him, strong and sturdy with a dark wisdom in his eyes I hadn't noticed before. It was a knowing glare in his face that seemed to say that he knew everything worth knowing about the world and could summon it at a moment's notice, the secret to his strength and success.

I wondered about his motive. Was he trying to hide something? Did he know something that I didn't? Who was I kidding? He could probably write a book on all the things he knew that I didn't.

There was something there but I couldn't put my finger on it, fear perhaps. Not the kind of fear that regular Joes like me feel, certainly not the kind of fear that I had experienced that day on Omaha Beach. This fear was subtle and aloof. The fear of being found out for what you are, the fear of responsibility, of being charged to protect something sacred and flimsy. The fear of watching over a family name and reputation, knowing full well you have almost no control over the outcome. It was like the guy placing the last card atop a house of cards, praying it won't come collapsing down around him.

"That's a lot of money," I remarked, opening the envelope and running my thumb across the edges of the bills.

"My family is very important to me."

I had handled a lot of dirty money in my day but this seemed dirtier than any I had ever held. I was struck with the thought that I'd rather take blood money from working stiffs trying to salvage their crummy lives, it seemed more noble.

"What exactly would I have to do?" Noble or not, it was a lot of money.

"Nothing, really, keep your eyes open, follow the investigation and the way it's heading. Keep me abreast as to what's happening. Poke around and see what you come up with. Most importantly, make sure I know what's going on at all times."

That's what he wanted. That's what old man Chilton always wanted, to know everything that was going on, to maintain control.

"Did you find out about that missing money?" I asked, stuffing the envelope in my jacket.

Chilton cleared his throat. "Why, yes, I did, actually. It turns out there was a rather large sum of money missing, around fifteen hundred dollars."

"How do you know?"

"I had my secretary run back to the office and check the safe."

"Dorothy?"

"Yes."

I wondered if the old man really wanted to know everything. I wondered if he wanted to know that I knew he was lying.

Chapter Fourteen

*C*hilton left first. I had another shot before taking my leave. From the bar, I wandered back up into the lobby. There still weren't many people. Aside from Dorothy, there was no one I knew.

Across the grand room, off to the side of the main desk and through the archway was another doorway that led to a series of small office rooms and conference areas reserved for the hotel staff and business functions. Standing outside, two deputies were shooting the breeze. It looked like something I might be interested in.

One of the other useful things they taught us at the Staley School was if you wanted to get into a place you weren't supposed to be to walk right in, brisk and determined, like you belonged, like you had a purpose. As far as the success rate for this procedure, I'd say, from experience, it works about thirty percent of the time. This time it worked.

They didn't bother to look up as I strolled by, still caught up in whatever it was they were talking about. Past them, down a narrow corridor I heard voices coming from a room on the left. The door was open and I went up and stood in the doorway.

Sheriff Talbert and a deputy had their backs to me, leaning over a small table. On the other side of the table sat Gilbert

Fleming. His eyes were wide and scared, sweat pouring down his face. They were interrogating him and it looked as though they were doing a pretty good job of it.

"Where were you when Tucker Morgan was killed?" Talbert asked, hard and sharp.

"I was in my room."

"Doing what?"

"I was sleeping."

"Anybody see you go in?"

"My sister, she walked me to my room before she went to hers."

At the risk of getting myself thrown out, I decided to throw in my two cents. "That's funny because Bradley says he walked Lucy to her room right before the murder."

They all turned to look at me, Gilbert nervous and frightened, the two cops angry and irritated.

"This is official police business," Talbert said.

"Maybe it was earlier." Gilbert offered, answering my question.

I ignored Talbert and stepped in, looking directly at Gilbert. "It doesn't really make sense that she would walk you up, go to her room and then go back downstairs just to walk back up with Bradley."

Talbert seemed to lose interest in me for the moment and turned back to Gilbert. "That seems a little far-fetched."

"Maybe she forgot something in her room."

I pressed on. "The other funny thing is I saw you coming back to your room at around six this morning, you had a pretty good load on. I'd say you had quite the time of it last night."

"I couldn't sleep. I went down to the hotel bar for a drink or two."

"You just keep getting funnier and funnier. You see, I was returning from the hotel bar and I don't remember seeing you."

"What's with that?" Talbert asked Gilbert.

"Ok, so I went off property for a drink."

"Where to?" the Sheriff snapped.

"A little place in town called the Sand Dollar Lounge."

"Anybody see you?"

"Lots of people."

"So why didn't you come clean with this up front?"

"I was there to meet a certain young lady. Let's just say we were trying to remain discreet."

"Anybody I know?"

Gilbert looked Talbert over. "I doubt it."

"This girl of yours got a name?"

Gilbert hesitated like he didn't want to answer. "Sally … Sally Devin."

"So, you and Miss Devin were there all evening?"

"Actually, it's Mrs. Devin and we were there for quite some time."

"So it's like that, is it?"

"I told you we were trying to be discreet."

"Did you ask him about the argument?" I asked Sheriff Talbert.

"Yeah, we did. It appears Tucker Morgan didn't approve of Gilbert's lifestyle."

"He called me a scoundrel."

"I'm guessing you've been called worse," I said. "Besides, 'you can't do that' isn't really the proper response when somebody calls you a name."

Talbert and his crony turned back to Fleming. Gilbert hesitated for a moment like he was trying to think of an excuse. He wasn't a very good liar.

"He threatened to go to my father and tell him all about the way I was living. My father is very old fashioned, he wouldn't approve with the way I live my life."

The two cops turned back to me, awaiting my next comment.

"From what I hear, Daddy knows all about your lifestyle choices and he's none too happy about it. In fact, from what I can tell, everybody in your circle knows of your reputation." Then to Talbert, "Gilbert here is a bit of a playboy hot shot living beyond his means, his antics are quite famous in these parts."

Talbert's glare was fixed on me, his expression one of suppressed fury. "You can go, Mr. Fleming. We'll talk more later. Make sure you don't stray too far."

The sheriff never took his eyes off me as Gilbert gathered

himself and rushed out the door. He now had me in his sights.

"What gives, I thought you weren't going to go snooping around?"

"I'm just a friend of the family, trying to help out." I was suddenly aware of the envelope of money in my jacket pocket and it felt like it was bulging out the front of my suit.

"Speaking of which, what's a grunt like you doing mixing it up with likes of the Chiltons?"

"I told you, I served with Bradley in the army."

"You seem to know an awful lot for an old army buddy."

"What can I say? I'm a perceptive guy."

"You've been in town, what, two days?"

"Yeah."

"And in two days you've got the scoop on the whole clan?"

"I don't know about that, but I'm starting to get a feel for how things work around here."

"I'd say you've got a lot more than a feel. It's almost as if you're an insider."

"I've got good ears."

"You're a little out of your element to be as firmly planted on the inside as you are."

"It must be my sparkling personality."

"There's something fishy about you, McKeller."

"About me? What about Gilbert Fleming? He's changed his story four times, has a flimsy alibi and has motive written all over him."

"You let me worry about that. We might not be as fancy as you city slickers from up north but we tend to get things done down here."

"You talk to Chilton about some missing money Tucker might have had on him?"

"Fifteen big ones, his secretary went back to the office and found it missing."

"Yeah, that's what I heard." I almost mentioned my talk with Dorothy Jackson, or White, or whatever she was going by today. I decided to keep it under my hat. It would be bad business to incriminate my new boss in the first fifteen minutes I was working for him.

"You ask a lot of questions for an innocent bystander."

"I'm a naturally curious kind of guy."

"Curiosity has a way of biting a guy in the ass sometimes."

"Thanks for the heads up. I'll keep that in mind."

"Look here, McKeller, in your travels, if you were to turn up any information pertinent to this investigation, you would be obligated to come forward. If not, it could be *misconscrewed* as withholding evidence."

"I get that. We've got the same laws in Baltimore."

"Just so we understand each other."

"I already gave you Gilbert on a silver platter. I caught him in four lies."

"We had Gilbert before you came in. We would have gotten it out of him."

Sure they would have. I nodded.

"You got anything else for me?" the sheriff asked.

I thought about it for a moment. There was the whole discrepancy with Chilton and Dorothy Jackson going back to the office and finding the missing cash. There was the way Lucy had blatantly lied about being with her brother, covering for him no doubt. There were my suspicions about my friend Bradley and Katherine Mathews, the odd things I had witnessed between them. There was even the jealous husband angle with Charley Jackson and the affair I suspected his wife might have had with Morgan.

All in all, I had a lot but none of it amounted to a hill of beans. I decided to do what any other fine, upstanding citizen would do.

"Sorry, Sheriff, I've got nothing. You know as much as I do."

"I know you're not actually investigating the matter, but if anything comes your way, give me a holler." His words were friendly on the surface but hinted to a festering despise for me barely underneath.

"Just so we understand each other." He said again.

Chapter Fifteen

*M*y talk with the sheriff left me feeling all warm and fuzzy inside. I felt like I needed to get out of the hotel for awhile. Even the luxury of the Ocean Forest could get a tad tiring to a regular muck like me. I could have strolled out the back door and into the sunshine, but I suspected the Atlantic was still out there and I wasn't ready to face her again.

Instead, I went up to Bradley's room and knocked. I needed a favor.

He seemed a bit scattered when he answered, like he'd just woken up or was in the middle of something else, or was expecting someone different to come knocking. It wasn't the first time I had witnessed odd behavior from him that weekend. The truth is there was a list of little things mounting up, mostly things I couldn't put my finger on. I figured all those roads led back to Katherine Mathews in some way.

"I need to borrow your car." I told him.

"My car?"

"I want to take a little ride into town, maybe take in the sights."

"There's not much else to see."

"Yeah, well, I just need to get out for awhile."

"Ok, no problem. I'll call down to the desk and have the car brought around for you."

"Thanks."

"Do you want me to go with you?"

"No, that's OK. I'll be fine."

He smiled his carefree smile. "Have fun."

Bradley went back to whatever he was doing and I went down to the front desk. A friendly, over polite guy in a vest and tie greeted me. "Can I help you, sir?"

"McKeller, to pick up Mr. Chilton's car."

"Yes sir, the car is waiting for you out front. Is there anything else I can do for you today?"

Everyone who worked at the Ocean Forest, with the possible exception of the elevator operator, was bend over backwards helpful, catering to the guests' every need. I had never been pampered in such a way.

I walked out the front door where a bellman was waiting beside Bradley's car, holding the door open for me. "Can I get anything else for you?" he asked as I climbed in.

"No thanks." I handed him a quarter, as I don't mind throwing money around for good service.

Pulling the car out of the hotel, I made a left onto Porcher Avenue, a two-way paved road that ran south, with the Atlantic Ocean off your left shoulder before linking up with the semi-paved Ocean Drive. Ocean Forest was also the name of the area the hotel sat square in the middle of, just south of something called Singleton Swash. The road was an eight-mile stretch that continued down toward Myrtle Beach proper, Floral Beach, Murrell's Inlet, toward Pawley's Island before giving way to dirt.

The road was meant to run the distance of the thirty-five mile stretch of beaches they called the Horry Strand, but when the war hit and building materials were rationed, completion of the road was postponed. It looked like they were just getting started at finishing the project.

Along the road were splattered small beach cottages, summer getaway spots for the working class, and the occasional Mom and Pop store. Couples and families wandered in and out of the area dressed in swimming attire, carrying towels and picnic baskets, strolling about like they hadn't a care in the world. It made me wonder if there wasn't something to this vacation thing.

As I drove through Myrtle Beach, the most expansive development on the coast, a small business district arose, more stores, picnic pavilions, a few small motels and a carnival center. I made a right and headed toward the downtown area, crossing over Kings Highway, a semi-finished road that had taken its name from an Indian trail settlers used to move goods north and south before the revolution. Calling it a highway was a stretch, at best. There was a post office, a bus stop and the Myrtle Beach Train Depot I came into town through.

There were a couple of paved roads running off to the west, one of them Hwy 503, the chief route to Conway, the next biggest town around, another called Main Street. Main Street shot off at an angle and was a row of connected brick buildings housing a drugstore, the Broadway Movie Theater and a few other shops with the Seven Seas Grill at one end and the Kozy Korner Grill at the other. It looked like any other Main Street in any other small town in America.

I stopped into the Kozy Korner for a cup of coffee. The place was clean, all white tile and linoleum with a mix of aluminum booths and small tables, homey and every bit as cozy as the name suggested. There were a few booths off to the side and a counter up front. I planted myself on a stool and ordered a cup of Joe from a small thin woman with dark ethnic features, Greek maybe. She was friendly in an all-business sort of way and made me feel more comfortable than any of the stuffed shirts I had been hobnobbing with for the past few days.

At one end of the room was a phone booth and I walked over and went in, picking up the phone book from under the shelf. The phone book barely qualified as a book and it was about half as thick as most pulp fiction novels you'd find. I paged through the back and found the listing for a Timothy and Sally Devin. They lived on a road called Palmetto Way.

Back at the counter, I finished off my coffee and laid two bits on the counter.

"Thank you, honey," the lady said as she scooped up my money and cleared my cup.

"No problem. Can you tell me how to find Palmetto Way?"

"Well, sure I can. It's just as easy as pie." She went on to give me directions, turn right at the end of main, down four blocks and take another right at the old Smith barn, hang a left at the old Cloisters house. I figured I had enough to get me close.

The Devins lived in a one story beach house in the middle of a barren block on a sand road. It was a bit tattered looking and in need of a new paint job but I had seen worse in my time. I walked up to the front door and knocked.

A blonde in a house coat opened the door slightly and peered out the crack. She looked a bit rough around the edges with her hair disheveled and dark circles around her eyes. I guessed with a little makeup and primping she could be quite a looker and it was apparent she was hiding a cute figure under the worn out house dress.

"Sally Devin?"

"Yeah?"

"I'm a friend of Gilbert Fleming."

Her eyes got wide and she looked around nervously, peeking past me and making sure I was alone. "I don't know any Gilbert Fleming."

"He knows you. He says he knows you pretty well."

"There must be some mistake."

"Is your husband home?"

The nervous on her face turned to panic but she tried to hide it as best she could. "No, he's working."

"Can I ask you a couple of questions?"

"I'm sorry but I'm very busy." She went to shut the door, but I stuck my foot in the way, preventing it from being slammed in my face.

"If you'd rather I could come back when Tim is home."

Sally stopped pushing on the door and let herself go limp in front of me. "What do you want?"

"I want to ask you a few questions and get out of your life forever." This seemed to relax her a little.

"I know Gilbert."

"I figured you did. When's the last time you saw him?"

"Look, mister, I'm a married woman ... "

"All the more reason to tell me what I want to know and get

95

rid of me."

"Me and my husband have been having some problems for awhile. I met Gilbert in a bar. He makes me laugh, shows me a good time. Is that a crime?"

"That depends on how good a time he shows you, what with you being married and all."

Her face went flush and she avoided looking me in the eye. "He's a high roller. I've never been with anyone like him before. He makes me feel special."

"I'm not really that interested in the whats and hows of you and Gilbert. What you do is your own business. I just want to know when you saw him last."

"I was with him last night."

"What time was that?"

"Around eleven or so, I guess. I met him at a bar."

"What bar?"

"The Sand Dollar Lounge."

"How late were you two there?"

"Late."

"Were you there the whole time?"

She hesitated. "Gilbert has a friend with a beach house close by. He lets him use it when he's not there. We got a bottle and went over for awhile."

"What time were you there till?"

"We were there all night. Gilbert left early this morning."

"Was Gilbert there the whole time? Did he leave for anything during the night, to get another bottle or something?"

I could tell she hated answering my questions. It was like having her teeth pulled out with pliers. "He never went anywhere. I was with him the whole night."

"How was Gilbert acting last night, did he seem agitated or anything?"

Sally took a deep breath. "He was pretty worked up. I guess he has this big deal in the works and he hit some sort of snag. He was pretty upset when he got to the bar."

"You know anything about this deal?"

She shook her head slowly from side to side. "You'd have to ask Gilbert about that."

I didn't believe her but decided not to delve any deeper about the business deal. Admitting to adultery was one thing, but blowing open a business deal that could set her and her boyfriend up later in life was another. There was no doubt in my mind that she knew more. Gilbert wasn't the kind of guy to keep stuff like that to himself, especially if it made him look like a big shot in the eyes of a pretty gal.

"There's liable to be some other people come asking around about Gilbert's whereabouts last night, cops and stuff. I'm guessing if you want to keep this under wraps you'd better cooperate as best you can."

"Is Gilbert in trouble?"

"Not if everything you've told me is true."

"Who are you?"

"I'm just a friend of the family. As far as I'm concerned my little visit doesn't have to become public knowledge. That goes both ways."

Sally nodded her understanding. I tipped my hat to her and walked away, back out to the car. I had one more stop to make.

Most of the other off shoot roads were dirt and sand, containing clusters of houses. Behind civilization were miles of thick forest and the occasional farm. Truck farms they called them and they were some of the largest in the Carolinas, shipping fresh fruits and vegetables all across the two states. You got the sense that you were in an agricultural center, giving way to the rush of tourism that invaded every year.

The town looked budding and semi-crowded but it was nearing the end of the summer season, and I imagined it would dry up soon as the vacationers headed back inland to their real lives. I guessed you could rent one of those places pretty cheap in a couple of month's time.

I followed some of the side roads in and out, searching for a needle in a haystack, albeit a pretty small haystack. I found what I was looking for after about ten minutes.

Housed in what didn't look like much more than a run-down shack, the Sand Dollar Lounge sat half a block off the main road, tucked in between two larger beach homes. There was a sand and oyster shell parking lot with enough space for three cars along side it.

Inside, the place was dark and damp, cluttered with tables, a small bar running down the left side. The walls were covered in sea shells and fishing nets, old photos of fishing boats, dried out star fish.

A young guy on the tall side of short stood behind the bar polishing glasses, talking with his two other customers, a couple of guys in Bermuda shorts and button up shirts. There was another guy sitting at a table in the far corner of the room but I couldn't make him out, my eyes still adjusting from the bright sunshine outside. The bartender flashed me a friendly smile as I came in.

"Howdy there, stranger," he said, "can I get you a drink?"

I ordered the usual.

He hesitated for a second like he was considering whether or not to serve me. I caught him glancing over and taking a peek at the empty shot glasses in front of his other customers. This was most likely not one of the designated spots where you could legally buy liquor and I figured he was weighing his options where I was concerned, deciding whether it was worth risking the fine.

"I'm not a cop," I assured him. This seemed to perk him up some.

"Tommy Shannon," he told me, introducing himself as he sat my drink in front of me. I took off my fedora and sat it on the bar.

"You ain't from around here, are you?" His voice was a touch on the gravelly side and his accent was thick and steady, less polished than the Southerners I'd been surrounded by for two days. He was a regular guy.

"No. I'm visiting from Baltimore."

"Baltimore, is that so?"

"Yeah, I'm staying at the Ocean Forest."

Tommy stopped what he was doing and shot me a funny look. "The Ocean Forest? Damn, that's a nice hotel."

I agreed.

"You know Sinatra stayed there?"

I didn't.

"Cagney too," one of the patrons informed me.

The other guy chimed in with, "My old man saw Tallulah Bankhead there once."

"Impressive."

"How is it?" Tommy asked.

"It's nicer than anything I've ever seen before."

The three laughed, slapping each other on the shoulders.

"A million bucks they spent on that thing," a guy told me.

"And that was in twenty-nine when a million bucks was a million bucks," Tommy added. "'The Castle in the Sand,' they call her."

The three laughed some more, taking turns telling me stories of the Ocean Forest, weddings and parties they'd attended there, packages they'd delivered, stories they'd heard second and third hand. It was strange to hear the devotion in their voices as they talked about the grand hotel, which was obviously above their means to visit on any kind of regular basis, like just having it in their community elevated all of them. There was a pride about them as they spoke of her as though she were a successful family member.

"You here on vacation?"

"No, I'm here for the Chilton wedding."

"Chilton? You know the Chiltons?"

"Yeah, you?"

"Never met any of them but I sure know about them. I guess everyone around here knows of the Chiltons."

"Hell, old man Chilton owns about half of everything in this town. He's also got one of the largest farm supply stores in the state. I guess most every farmer in the county buys from Chiltons," another guy said.

"What he doesn't own he's buying up."

"He was part of the airbase deal too."

"The airbase?" I asked.

"The Myrtle Beach airbase," Tommy explained. "They built it back in forty-one, used it as a training station for bombers. Nowadays it's used as a redeployment center for veterans. They bring the fellows back here and retrain them for duty assignments in the Pacific. We still got a lot of guys over there."

"The old man used to own it?"

"He used to own part of it, anyway. He made a bundle on that deal, I'll bet."

"Chilton pretty much runs the beach?"

Tommy thought about it a second. "He's one of the big boys but he's not the biggest. Myrtle Beach Farms is pretty big and Burroughs and Collins own the bulk of it, they control most of the coastline but Chilton's got a big chunk of the inland stuff. He owns a lot."

"Imagine the kind of money Chilton's going to make once they put in that highway," a guy suggested.

"What highway is that?" I asked.

Tommy grinned. "There's talk that they're thinking of running a highway straight up to North Carolina and all the way down to Charleston. They say they're going to link it up north with other highways. We're talking two lanes paved the whole way. A road like that would make travel here a lot easier. It would bring in a lot more folks."

"When's this supposed to happen?"

"I don't know exactly. It's mostly just talk for now."

"You guys know a fellow named Gilbert Fleming?"

The three looked at each other a bit uneasy. "We know Gil."

"Did you work last night?" I asked Tommy. "Was he in here?"

"Yeah, Gil was here."

"About what time was that?"

Tommy gave me a funny look. "You sure you ain't some kind of copper?"

I shrugged my shoulders. "No, I told you, I'm down for the wedding. I met Gilbert at the hotel. He was the one who told me about this place."

He nodded. "He was in here kind of late, around eleven or so. You a friend of Gil's?"

"I just met the guy. He seems like an alright bloke."

"Just don't lend him any money," one of the others said with a chuckle.

"I thought he had plenty of money. Isn't his family loaded?"

"His family's got some money but that don't mean Gilbert's got any."

The bartender cut in. "Look, I don't know how well you know Gilbert but a piece of advice, watch your back with that one. He's into everybody around here for a chunk of change. I'm guessing I've got forty or fifty bucks in bar tabs back there with his name on them."

"If he's a bad pay, why do you keep running him tabs?"

"Call it an investment," the other guy said. "He's fixing to come into some money here soon and we're all getting paid back."

"How do you know?"

"We've seen it," another guy added. "He showed us …"

Tommy cut him off. "We just know is all. We've known Gil near all our lives. He might have a wild hair but we've known him a long time. He wouldn't do us like that."

"So, he's got something in the works?"

"I wouldn't know anything about that. A man's business is his own business." Tommy seemed a little less friendly than before.

"Last night, was he here with a girl?"

One of the guys laughed and said, "Gil's always here with a girl."

"This girl named Sally Devin?"

Tommy was staring me down. "You sure ask a lot of questions."

"Just curious, I guess."

"Look, a guy comes in here, maybe he's with a certain young lady, and maybe he comes to a spot like this because he doesn't want to be recognized. What business is it of mine who comes in with who?"

"Does that mean Gilbert was here with Mrs. Devin or not?"

"You want another drink?" He was changing the subject.

"Sure."

Tommy poured me another and walked away, back over to his regulars. They were huddled up in the corner and talking amongst themselves. I was no longer a part of the conversation and it seemed they were purposely talking low enough to keep me from hearing.

Nursing my drink, I glanced around the room. My eyes had adjusted to the darkness and I was seeing it clear for the first time. The place was old and haggard looking, the kind of place working stiffs tend to gather. It made me wonder why a guy like

101

Gilbert Fleming would choose to hang there.

I glanced over my shoulder to the guy sitting alone at the table. He had a shot and a beer in front of him with four more empty shot glasses lined up behind them. The guy was staring off into the distance with a look on his face like he wasn't actually seeing anything, like he was deep in thought. It was Charlie Jackson.

Tossing a few bucks on the bar, I picked up my drink and hat and walked over to the table. He didn't seem to notice me approach.

"Mind if I have a seat?"

Charlie Jackson looked up at me with blurry eyes. He didn't recognize me. "I'd rather you didn't."

Ignoring him, I sat down across the table. "Do you remember me?"

He tried to make me out but he was having a tough go of it. "Should I?"

"We met at the hotel bar last night. I was talking with Dorothy."

Jackson's face turned red and seemed to clench up. His puffy hands pulled into fists and his body went rigid and tense. "What do you want?"

"I just thought we could talk, is all."

"I'm kind of busy at the moment."

"Yeah, I see that. I thought maybe you and I could have a little chat before the police have to get involved."

"Police what? I didn't do nothing."

"I never said you did."

"What do you want to talk about?"

"Dot and Tucker Morgan for starters."

Charlie bit down on his bottom lip. "What's that supposed to mean?"

"Nothing. They worked together, right?"

"Yeah."

"They were pretty good friends from what I understand."

"If you've got something to say, spit it out."

"I'm just saying, they worked together for a long time. They worked along side each other day in and day out … "

"You got a point to all this?"

"You didn't like Tucker, did you?"

Jackson didn't answer, just sat there glaring at me.

"Ever get jealous of the two of them?"

Still no answer.

"I imagine it must have been tough. Those two always together, working long hours, late nights in the office ..."

Charlie Jackson was pretty quick for his age. Maybe I was just slow for mine. He was up in an instant, leaning across the table and whirling around with a roundhouse that caught me on the side of the jaw. I tumbled back across my chair and found myself lying on the ground, looking up at him. He was in a fighting stance, perched to come at me again the second I got up, his face a dark purple.

"Did I hit a nerve?"

"Don't you talk like that! Dotty and Tucker worked together, that's all."

"What's wrong, Charlie? Did you get a little upset with all the Tucker talk at home? Were you afraid they were spending a few too many late nights at the office?"

"You don't know what you're talking about. There was nothing between Dot and Tucker. They worked together is all."

"It still made you angry, though, didn't it?"

I had pulled myself up to a sitting position, resting on my left arm, my right at the ready in case he came for me again.

"Sure I was jealous. Who wouldn't be? Tucker was classy and sophisticated; he was a smart guy like in those books she always reads. I'm just some lug that works with his hands. The way she used to go on about him all the time made me crazy. Tucker this, Tucker that ..."

"How angry did it make you, Charlie? Angry enough to kill Tucker Morgan?"

Jackson stopped in his tracks. His face froze over and his body seemed immobilized with shock. "Kill Tucker Morgan, are you crazy?"

Tommy and the other boys from the bar were over by this time. They helped me to my feet but not in a gentle way. "We don't want no trouble." Tommy said.

One of them handed me my fedora but not in a gentle way. The other two were pushing me back toward the front door. "Is that all you got, Charlie?" I shouted over them. "You want to tell me where you were last night?"

"All right, that's enough." Tommy said, still pushing me back. "You need to go and don't come back."

At the door they stopped pushing and I gathered myself together, straightening my jacket and placing my hat on my head. "Thanks for the Southern hospitality."

"Don't let the door hit you where the good Lord split you." The bartender said but not in a gentle way.

Chapter Sixteen

*O*utside the sunlight was blinding and the afternoon heat was all but unbearable. To top it off, my jaw was aching. Charlie Jackson had a pretty good right hook. As I got to the car, I got more good news. The driver's side front tire was flat. When it rains it pours.

I walked around to the back of the car and popped the trunk. Digging through the rubble, I rooted around for the jack and spare. Stuffed near the back was a leather briefcase and I pulled it out and started to stick it off to the side, out of the way. Something stopped me.

Maybe it's the snoop in me, another hazard of the job. Maybe it was all the questions swirling through my head. Either way, it seemed like a good idea to pry into my best friend's personal belongings. What can I say? I'm a jerk like that.

Inside I found a bunch of papers that meant almost nothing to me, real estate contracts and perspectives, a ton of boring documents pertaining to his everyday work. It was about as interesting as reading the phone book for fun.

Underneath the various folders and loose papers I found a map and I pulled it out and unfolded it. Done in bright greens and yellows, it was a map of Myrtle Beach and surrounding areas going from Wilmington, North Carolina down to Charleston, South

Carolina. It gave a sense of just how much of the county was un-tapped, most of it green and unmarked, small towns and out coves indicated in black, spread out sporadically down the coast.

In red ink, running parallel to the coastline was a hand drawn line. It followed the same route as Ocean Drive and Kings High-way but this one ran the length of the map traveling down the entire Horry Strand and then some. It sat closer to the coast and looked to be less than a mile off the water, stretching through mostly green virgin land and the occasional farm. Beside it, scribbled in haphazard lettering was the abbreviation, Hwy.

Even a dumb muck like me could figure out it was the pro-posed highway that Tommy the bartender had mentioned earlier.

Along side it, just to the left of the Myrtle Beach designa-tion, someone had drawn a large oval, still in red ink. Inside the circle they had written Fleming. Just to the side of that oval was a slightly larger area, more rectangular, with the Fleming land sit-ting between it and the highway. This patch was marked Mathews. Behind the Mathews patch an even bigger area was marked off, still farther away from the proposed road with both the Fleming and Mathews plots between it and the thin red line. This area was twice as big as the others, stretching out to the north and curling up around the other two, almost like it was on the verge of swal-lowing them up. This one was marked Chilton.

I stuffed the map back into the briefcase, trying to put all the stuff in the way I had found it. Next, I dug down into the trunk and pulled out the spare tire and jack. Taking off my hat and jacket, I rolled up my sleeves and went about changing the tire.

It's not that I'm opposed to hard work and, truth be told, changing a tire isn't all that hard but by the time I finished I was spent. The South Carolina heat was like nothing I had ever felt, the air thick and wet, the heavy sunlight baking the back of my head and neck. By the time I was done, my shirt was soaked through and I felt like I was covered in a layer of sweat. My first impulse was to head back into the bar for a cool drink but I decided that wasn't the best idea I'd had all day.

I didn't even bother to put my hat and jacket back on, toss-ing them into the passenger seat and climbing in. I started her up and headed off to the west, to what would have been the left of

Myrtle Beach on the map.

Less than a mile in, I turned right onto a dirt road. There was nothing much around but trees and tall grass. From the opposite direction came an old man on a tractor. He was wearing faded overalls with no shirt and his skin was the darkest of browns, rough and leathery, his receding hair short, white and curly. The old man shot me a friendly smile as we crept past each other. I even managed to smile back.

Bradley's car wasn't made for dirt roads and I prodded her along, barely touching the accelerator. She hummed along, steady and true, but I got the sense that she wanted me to gun her, daring me to open her up and see what she was capable of. You didn't see many machines like her on the streets of Baltimore.

It was difficult for me to fathom that he'd even lent me this beautiful car. If I were him I wouldn't let a mug like me wash it.

I picked a spot and pulled her over to the side of the road. The country was pristine and untouched, hulking trees with dipping limbs, leaves flowing down in clumps like water rolling off a rock. Tall, majestic shrubs, weaving in the breeze, with large buds perched on top, looking like soldiers marching in formation.

There were strange birds flocking about. They were white with long beaks and longer necks, skinny legs they tucked in behind them as they took flight with wide outstretched wings. When they were on the ground, they pranced about in small pockets of water, taking exaggerated steps on their thin, stick-like limbs, oblivious to me watching them.

They weren't the only birds. There were large hawks circling over head and something that might have been an eagle flying past, gliding along, its intimidating wingspan stretched across the horizon, floating through the air like he was surveying his kingdom. It pumped its wings twice and picked up speed, taking off in another direction and disappearing into the wilderness.

Out of the car, I walked around, into the tree line. The ground was soft and wet, giving way to my feet with every step, sinking around the sides of my shoes as I trudged in farther.

It wasn't swampland, not the kind you see in Tarzan movies, anyway. There was water everywhere but it seldom looked like it got much deeper than a foot or so. Rolling grass ran through it,

107

sometimes growing directly out of the water, other times forming on small dry banks spattered along the edges. Tree roots broke the surface on occasion, big thick ones that looked like floating logs skimming the top.

Everything around me felt alive and the air was filled with the sounds of singing birds, rustling leaves and running water. There were even small lizards here and there, bright green and the size of a man's forefinger, scampering across leaves and tree trunks, quick and frenzy-like.

This had to be it. I had to be standing in the middle of the land that belonged to Herbert Fleming. If not, I had to be very close, on land that resembled it a great deal. Somewhere beyond the dense foliage and dark recesses of the forest, out of sight, would be the Mathews land. I imagined it wouldn't look much different.

From off my left shoulder I heard something move, a splash or a rustle. I took a few steps over to see what it was, the water now seeping into my socks. There was a high plant with wide green leaves the size of footballs blocking my view so I went over and brushed it aside, peering past.

I wasn't prepared for what I saw. I don't know how anybody could be prepared for a sight like that.

My body froze and I felt the wind leave my lungs like I had been kicked in the gut. Terror shot through my brain and I stood gawking, trembling like a small child, unable to even comprehend what I was looking at. Nobody warned me about the gators.

There, not four feet away from me, lying in the dirt and grass, just barely out of the water, was the largest reptile I ever saw. If it wasn't seven foot long it wasn't an inch.

It was facing me, black eyes protruding out its skull and staring me down. The nose was long and pointed, the mouth closed but huge jagged teeth visible in its grin. The body was wide and rippled, like it was wearing some impenetrable armor that scoured down the surface of it. The tail was thick and looked long enough to whip around and hit me in the face.

I took a step backward and let go of the branch I was peeking over, losing sight of the monster. Another step backward, the muck sucking my shoes into the wet. Another step, slow and easy, trying to be as quiet as possible, trying to control my breathing and pulling my thoughts into some kind of logical order.

There was a sound. I'm not sure what it was but I wasn't about to stick around and find out. I took off running, tripping over a tree root and falling face first into the mud. There was no way I was going to stop moving. Fighting my way to my feet, I ran faster than I knew I was capable of moving. Off balance and disoriented, I sprinted for the tree line, stumbling and fighting my way through the brush and water.

I was back at the car before I ever turned back to see if anything was chasing me. There was no sign of the alligator.

For a few moments I stood by the side of the car, catching my breath, surveying the area I had just come from, looking for the hideous beast. I was soaked with water, covered in mud from head to toe and my left shoe was missing, my white sock brown and drenched, barely clinging to my foot.

From the south I heard a motor and I looked up to see the old black man on the tractor making his way back up the road. As he passed me, he gave me his friendly grin again, this time much larger than the one he'd shown me before.

"You be careful back there, lots of gators around," he said with a chuckle.

"I'll keep that in mind."

Maybe it was my imagination but I thought I could hear him laughing all the way down the road. I got back in the car and headed back to the Ocean Forest.

Chapter Seventeen

*T*he valet met me out front of the hotel. He walked over and reached to open the door, but he seemed a bit timid, like he didn't want to touch the car.

I got out and looked back. The white car was now a dirty brown, covered in dust and filth, mud puddling in the front seat where I had been sitting.

Like nothing was out of the ordinary, I put my hat on and straightened my tie. "Do you think you could get this washed for me?"

"Yes sir."

I handed him a wet quarter with my muddy hand and the kid stood there looking at it in the palm of his, unsure what to do with it.

"Thanks, I'd appreciate it."

From there I limped into the Ocean Forest lobby on one shoe, tracking mud and water behind me as I went, ignoring the looks I was getting from both the guests and workers of the hotel. What are you going to do?

Freckled Face stared at me sideways, as though he were dying to grill me about what happened on the way up to the third floor, but I wasn't about to give him the satisfaction. I stood my ground and stared blankly at the elevator doors as we ascended, determined to play it off like it was another day at the office.

"Have a nice day," he said to me as I exited. His voice was shrill and cocky and I could hear the amusement in his tone.

"Yeah, you too." The little punk. I guess going up and down in a four foot box all day tends to create attitude.

Back in my room I got cleaned up and changed into my other suit. I took the dirty one down to the front desk and they sent it out to be cleaned. The Ocean Forest was a full service hotel and you got the idea that there wasn't much that couldn't be arranged or taken care of from that front desk.

There were still a couple of hours to go before dinner, so I figured I'd wander around and kill some time. I worked my way through the lobby and out the back where we had all met for breakfast earlier.

Most of the guests were off on the beach or partaking in the other leisurely activities the resort offered, and only a few tables were taken. One of them was taken by Lucy and her father. They were having tea.

"Hello," I said as I approached.

"Hello." Lucy threw me a strained smile. She introduced me to her father and he invited me to join them.

She was wearing a navy blue summer dress, trimmed in white, a thin matching blazer over it. Conservative and classy, it made her look older and more refined than I was used to seeing. Her father was wearing a brown suit.

"I'm afraid I should apologize, Frankie. I've been a bit rude to you as late."

"Not at all, I completely understand."

Herbert Fleming looked confused.

"Mr. McKeller was asking a few questions about Gilbert after this whole dreadful affair began and I may have been a tad defensive," she explained.

The elder Fleming sat upright in his chair, even more so than usual, and wrinkled his brow. "Gilbert?"

I shrugged. "It comes with the job, nothing personal."

"Mr. McKeller is a private investigator out of Baltimore."

"Is that so?"

"After Tucker Morgan was murdered, he was inquiring

111

about Gilbert's whereabouts, what with the argument they'd had and all."

Fleming gave me a hard glare. "I can assure you that my son had nothing to do with the unfortunate set of events."

"I never said he did. I was just trying to point out that, in light of the circumstances, he might want to be as upfront with the police as possible. We certainly wouldn't want anyone thinking he was hiding anything."

"Certainly not," he agreed. "No doubt you've heard certain things regarding Gilbert. I will be the first to admit that he has a tendency for making bad decisions at times but he is definitely not a criminal."

"All the more reason for him to come forward with everything he knows."

"Gilbert has already come forward. He talked to the police earlier today," Lucy said.

"I know. I was there."

"What were you doing there?"

"I just kind of wandered in."

"Then you know that Gilbert had nothing to do with Tucker's untimely demise," Mr. Fleming added.

"I know that he was pretty shook up."

"Who wouldn't be?"

"Tell me, Mr. Fleming, does Gilbert work with you?"

Fleming looked a little uncomfortable, maybe stiffer than before. "No, Gilbert is self-employed."

"But he has interests within the family?"

"Naturally, Gilbert is an heir to the family holdings and as such has a stake in the family business."

"What is the family business? What exactly is it you do, Mr. Fleming?"

"At present, I am charged with overseeing the family estate."

I lit a smoke. "And just how is the family estate these days?"

"That's a tad personal, isn't it, Mr. McKeller?"

Lucy said, "I'm guessing that Frankie has been listening to some of the local gossip floating around, Father."

"People do tend to talk."

"Some people are under the impression that our family

is in some sort of dire straits but I can assure you that is far from true. Father has had a run of bad luck where business is concerned but — "

"I don't see where this is anyone's concern," Fleming interjected.

"No, Father, let's get this out in the open," Lucy replied. "Our family may not have the wealth of the Chiltons but we are doing just fine, thank you very much."

"If not having the Chilton's money was a crime, most of us would be guilty," I added.

"Money isn't everything."

"This is true, but it makes Sunday brunches at the country club more pleasant."

"Our family's financial situation is none of your business." The old man was cross with me, as cross as he got, I guessed.

"You are right about that, Mr. Fleming. It's just with my best friend getting married and a murderer on the loose, I tend to want to know what's going on around me."

Lucy's face tightened. "If you are implying that I'm marrying Bradley for his money — "

"No, Lucy, that's not where I was going with this at all."

She stared hard into my eyes, those emerald green gems in her eye sockets fixed to mine, deadly serious. "I have been in love with Bradley Chilton all of my life. I've never wanted anything more than to become his wife."

I believed her.

"Where were you when he and Katherine were an item?"

"See here now," Fleming said, standing up and tossing a white linen napkin on the table. "Such talk is highly inappropriate on the weekend of my daughter's wedding. I will not stand for such rude behavior in her presence."

Lucy's glare was still locked on mine. "We all have a past, Frankie. Katherine is a part of Bradley's. She's a part of mine as well. I've been friends with her for as long as I can remember."

"It must have eaten you alive to see them together, in love with him as you've always been."

"I demand you change the topic of this conversation," her father scolded me.

113

Lucy and I both ignored him and continued to talk, never looking away from each other.

"I always knew I was destined to be with Bradley. I was never worried for a minute. I knew that, in time, he would come around and see that we were meant to be together. What he and Katherine had was the kind of thing that stems from immaturity."

"Puppy love?"

"Exactly. Nothing at all like what Bradley and I have together."

"Just the same, it's a little odd isn't it, all of you such good friends?"

Lucy gave just a hint of a smile. "If I didn't know any better I'd think you were trying to pick a fight with me, Frankie."

"Not at all," I said. "I'm not stupid. I know I wouldn't stand a chance in that fight."

She let herself smile the rest of the way. "Frankie, I'm not a jealous person by nature. What's done is done. The important thing is that Bradley and I are together now. I'm not about to throw away a lifetime friendship over something that happened in the past."

I figured I had taken the conversation about as far as it was going to go so I looked up at Herbert Fleming. "I understand Gilbert has some kind of big deal in the works. You must be very proud."

Herbert and Lucy looked at each other with confused expressions. Then they looked back at me.

"Gilbert always has something in the works," Lucy said.

Herbert Fleming reached down and took his daughter by the arm, helping her out of her seat. "Mr. McKeller, I don't know how they do things where you're from, but down here we conduct ourselves with a certain amount of decorum. I suggest you brush up on your manners."

He sure told me.

The two of them nodded their goodbyes and left me sitting alone at the table. I watched as they made their way across the terrace, arm in arm, Mr. Fleming guiding his daughter along. He needn't have bothered. From where I was sitting, it looked like Lucy Fleming could more than take care of herself.

114

As they reached the door, Mrs. Fleming came strolling out, all smiles and sunshine. Lucy kissed her mother on the cheek and continued inside with her father. There was no kiss from Mr. Fleming but I figured that was par for the course. He wasn't a kissing in public kind of fellow.

Lydia Fleming glided across the patio like she was on stage, the proud mother of the bride and star of the weekend show. She smiled and bowed to passers-by and graciously waved to the people around as though she were the hostess of the party and the Ocean Forest Hotel her home.

She settled into a table a few down from mine and ordered something from a passing waiter.

I felt like I was on a pretty good roll as far as information gathering goes, even though none of it really added up to squat. Remembering what Katherine had told me about Lydia Fleming, I figured gossip central was the next logical stop. If I was looking for information there wasn't a better place to go.

"Hello, Mrs. Fleming."

She looked up at me with a bright smile, a lost look in her eye. "How do you do?"

"I'm a friend of your son-in-law to be," I said with a grin. "I just had tea with your husband and daughter."

"How nice to meet you," she beamed back.

Katherine wasn't kidding about Lucy's mom. In my first ten minutes sitting there I barely got a word in. She went on and on about people I had never heard of, places I'd never been and various happenings I had no connection with. My mind was swirling with useless information and I kept waiting for a break in the conversation.

One of the things she discussed was the murder of Tucker Morgan. While she didn't know anything more than I did, she did mention that word had it Tucker was having an affair with a married woman. She wasn't at liberty to say with whom but she suspected it might be someone affiliated with Chilton Real Estate. We both knew she was talking about Dorothy Jackson.

Finally, I had to interrupt if I was going to get a word in edgewise.

"Are you excited about Bradley joining the family?"

"Of course, Bradley is a lovely boy."

"And the families get along well?"

"Why yes, we've known each other for years."

"What about Mrs. Chilton? I haven't had a chance to get to know her."

Lydia let out a sigh. "The poor dear, such a lovely woman. It's a shame the way things turned out with her."

"How's that?"

She glanced around and leaned in toward me. "They say it's the rheumatism, but don't you believe it for a minute. It's nerves."

"Nerves?"

"And no wonder what that man put her through over the years."

"Mr. Chilton?"

Lydia nodded slowly. "You should have met her when we were younger, so carefree and full of life."

"What did he do?"

"What didn't he do? Alfred Chilton sucked the life out of her with his controlling. He drove the poor dear half out of her mind."

"He does like being in charge, doesn't he?"

"You have no idea. Alfred Chilton ruled over every little thing she did, the way she talked, dressed, behaved in public ..." She took a deep breath and shook her head side to side. "She never had a moment's peace. Alfred ruled over her like she was a belonging."

"And that sent her over the edge?"

"You didn't hear this from me but ... there was a man."

"A man?" Now we were getting to the juicy stuff.

"Bradley was still a young boy when she met him. He was everything that Alfred Chilton wasn't. She fell madly in love."

"Mrs. Chilton had a fling?"

"He was a wonderful man, handsome, intelligent, funny ..."

"What happened?"

"What do you think happened? Alfred put a stop to it."

"It must have been quite a scandal."

"Not really, Alfred shoved the whole thing under the carpet. He wasn't about to let a thing like that get out. The only reason I know is because we were such good friends at the time. Harriet used to confide everything to me."

"So Mr. Chilton put an end to the affair."

"Things were never the same after that. I don't think she ever recovered from the heartbreak. After that, Alfred became very cruel with her. He literally drove her out of her mind."

"Whatever became of the man?"

Lydia Fleming shrugged her shoulders. "I don't know. No one ever heard of him again. He simply vanished."

"Vanished? Isn't that a little odd?"

"Well, he wasn't from around here. I suppose he just went back to wherever he was from. Atlanta, I think."

"So, you never suspected any kind of foul play?"

Lydia laughed like I had said something ridiculous. "Foul play, what kind of people do you think we are down here?"

"I just thought …"

"Heavens, Mr. McKeller, I think you watch too many movies. I'm sure Alfred Chilton had something to do with his disappearance, but I'm positive it was nothing like that. Knowing Alfred the way I do, I imagine he threw a large sum of money at the problem."

"Afterward, Mrs. Chilton became depressed?"

"At first it was very subtle. She withdrew somewhat but we still saw her socially. She was just a bit more reserved than usual. Over the years, she withdrew more and more."

"Did Bradley know what was going on?"

"I doubt it. He was very young at the time. Harriet was always so wonderful with Bradley. They were very close when he was growing up. I guess as he got older she had less to do with his life and Alfred began to take a more active role in his upbringing. That's when she really began to get worse. She didn't have anything else to live for."

"Do you think Bradley blames his father for his mother's condition?" I asked.

"I would imagine so, everyone else does, but I've never heard him mention anything about it. Of course, they have a somewhat strained relationship, as I'm sure you've observed."

"Do you remember his name, the man she was seeing?"

Mrs. Fleming thought about it for a second, like she was searching the dark recesses of her mind for a name she hadn't thought of in years. "I believe it was Michael something ... Michael Tate, I think."

"How are things on your family front?" I said, guiding the conversation away from Harriet Chilton.

Lydia flashed me her trademark grin. "Things are absolutely lovely. We couldn't be happier for Lucy."

"How are things with Gilbert?"

Her smile faded a bit but she forced it to remain on her face. "Gilbert is just fine."

"I understand he has a big deal he's working on."

"I'm afraid Gilbert doesn't confide in his mother on such matters. I wouldn't know."

"Does Gilbert have much of a hand in the family business?"

"Oh no, that is strictly Herbert's department."

"It's kind of funny that Herbert doesn't include Gilbert on matters involving the family fortunes."

She looked a little uneasy for the first time. "I'm sure Herbert will bring Gilbert in when the time is right. Gilbert is just a bit of a free spirit at present."

"Your husband prefers to run things himself; there's nothing wrong with that. I get the sense Alfred Chilton does things pretty much the same way."

"Nonsense, Herbert is nothing like Alfred Chilton. In fact, there was a time when Herbert was a very generous and trusting man. He only took sole control over the family assets when ..." She stopped short, realizing she might be giving away too many family secrets.

"When what?" I asked, trying to pry it out of her.

"It was nothing, really. It's just that he had a business partner at one time. Herbert did so much for that man, much more than anyone else would have."

"And this man stabbed him in the back?"

The smile was all but gone from Lydia's face. "Let's just say that Herbert was trusting to a fault. He probably had too much confidence in ... him."

"This guy, was he another family member?"

"Lord no, he was a business acquaintance and a long time friend. I suppose that's where Herbert made his mistake, trusting anyone outside the family. That's not a mistake he will ever make again."

"Going outside the family?" I asked.

Lydia's smile gradually grew back. "I hope I haven't given you the wrong impression. It's not nearly the situation I'm making it out to be. It was just an unfortunate set of circumstances that happened some time ago. I can assure you that our family recovered quite nicely from the setback."

"I'm guessing that an experience like that leaves scars."

"Well, like I said, Herbert learned his lesson about doing business outside the family."

"That's good news for Gilbert."

"Gilbert has his own way of doing things. He's quite fine doing what he's doing."

"There's always Bradley, your new son-in-law."

"Mr. McKeller, you certainly do have an interest in our family concerns."

"What can I say? I'm the curious type. It's just that everyone is so warm and friendly, I like getting to know everyone."

"Well, of course, we like getting to know you too. Why don't you tell me a little about yourself?"

I gave Lydia Fleming a long hard look. She was a nice enough old gal and I'd had more unpleasant conversations in my time. As far as getting into the details of me, I wasn't really in the mood. Besides, I'd gotten enough out of her for one sitting. I still wasn't sure what I had, if anything, but I was sure that I was done with Lydia Fleming for the time being.

"I'd love to stay and chat, but I've really got to be running along."

She looked a little stunned at my abrupt exit, and I left her sitting alone at the table on the terrace of the Ocean Forest. It was the first time since we'd met that she wasn't speaking.

The whole Michael Tate thing was stuck in my head. It seemed a little fishy the way he upped and disappeared. I wondered what really happened to him. I wondered if Michael Tate hadn't somehow ended up as gator bait.

119

Chapter Eighteen

Call me crazy but I was beginning to enjoy my new role. For the first time ever, I was feeling like a real live detective, snooping around, asking questions, gathering information. The problem was I had no idea what I was actually doing.

On top of that, I was gathering a lot of information but none of it seemed to fit together and even less of it seemed to have anything to do with the murder of Tucker Morgan. So far, all I was getting was dirty laundry, something there was no shortage of in Myrtle Beach.

I wandered around the hotel for awhile, trying to figure out what to do next but I was coming up empty. My Staley School education was falling short, and I had no idea what my next move should be. All I knew was I had a fat pocket of money, and I was investigating something that had nothing to do with the unlawful pairings of the un-betrothed or the whereabouts of Rover.

I decided to go back up to my room and freshen up, regroup and get my thoughts together. While I was waiting for the elevator, the doors opened and out stepped a tall, broad shouldered man in a black suit.

He didn't seem to notice me as he walked by, toward the main entrance.

I had seen him once before. He was the guy who had been

sitting next to Old Man Chilton in the bar. I wondered if it wasn't Chet Bowman, the guy Dorothy Jackson had mentioned, the one who worked as some kind of strong arm or errand boy for Chilton.

Maybe I was feeling cocky, what with my big time case and all. Maybe I was desperate to figure out what was going on and eager to prove I was worth my salt as a private eye. Maybe I was just stupid.

I decided to follow him. It was early evening and I still had hours before the big dinner.

Out front of the hotel, he climbed into the driver's seat of a blue Ford sedan. I hailed a cab that was parked out in the circular driveway. It was then I got to say something that I'd always wanted.

"Follow that car."

The blue sedan took a right and headed north. My cabbie was following at around thirty yards behind. I kept telling the cabbie to lag further behind but he wasn't too interested in the fine art of tailing an automobile. He was too busy telling me about the local landmarks and the natural beauty Myrtle Beach had to offer.

We traveled for about six or seven miles before the sedan hung a right and headed toward the Ocean. There was a sign off to the side that announced we were entering an area called Atlantic Beach.

"Are you sure you want to go here?" the cabbie asked me.

"Yeah, why not?"

"Well, for one thing, you've got the wrong color skin."

Atlantic Beach was lodged in between Windy Hill and Crescent Beach, sitting on the ocean, a narrow strip of dirt road hosting a few shops, bars, night spots and food stands, surrounded by small beach houses and a couple of two-bit hotels. It was a big time resort for people who didn't have the money to go to a big time resort. It was a resort for people who didn't know what one was supposed to look like, and had the wrong color skin to get into one if they did. They called it The Black Pearl.

Segregated off from the surrounding communities, it was even billed in local brochures as a "popular resort for Negroes"

121

and it was where our darker brothers and sisters came to get away from the drudgery of their everyday lives, basking in the summer sun. It featured all the amenities you would find in its white counterpart, but there was something smaller scale and rundown about it.

Coming from inner city Baltimore, I wasn't used to seeing people separated off in such a blatant manner, although, even in Baltimore, coloreds and whites tended to keep to themselves. Me, I didn't have a problem with anyone due to the color of their skin. The truth is I knew plenty of colored people and I tended to dislike them about the same as most of the white people I knew.

The blue sedan pulled up in front of a little juke joint called Mack's Dive and the man in black made his way inside. I had the cabbie let me off at the corner and I walked back up to the place.

The street was much more crowded than that of Myrtle Beach and there was an energy about the place her sister town lacked. People frolicked about, laughing and joking, hanging in clusters, everyone having a good time. There was a family atmosphere about it but not in a kid friendly kind of way, more in an everybody-seemed-to-know-everybody way.

Everything about Atlantic Beach was different. As you walked down the road you were struck with the smell of food cooking, local delicacies like bar-b-cue pork, deep fried fish and collard greens. The smell was rich and boisterous, and even though the foods were foreign to me it made my stomach rumble with hunger.

The sounds were different from Myrtle Beach as well. Music seemed to be coming from various directions, low and rhythmic, strong and fiery, blaring from phonographs, radios and live guitars. It was the down and dirty sound of country blues and it lingered in the sizzling air, fusing itself into the landscape and igniting energy in the people it touched. It was like it was supplying the soundtrack for the lives of the community, sweltering hotter than the South Carolina sun.

Outside of Mack's Dive was a small chalkboard proclaiming someone called Blind Eye Regis would be playing there tonight. It also made mention of a special they were running on Red Hots, whatever they were.

It looked like things got off to an early start in Atlantic Beach as the joint was already crowded and the live music had begun. The sun was just beginning to set.

Inside, the place was alive and vibrant. People crowded the tables and dance floor, moving, shaking, cutting up all around me. On stage, an old black man in a worn out suit strummed hard on an acoustic guitar, his gravely voice rising above the noisy room. He was singing something about his baby running off with another man and leaving him alone and blue, his guitar his only faithful companion. I thought for a second about giving him my card.

I spotted the man in black across the barroom at a table. He was sitting with a young dark skinned man in blue jeans and a white pullover shirt. The man in black was calmly listening while the younger man seemed to be arguing, animated and passionate, waving his arms and pleading his case.

I took a seat at the bar and continued to watch the two, ordering a shot of whiskey from the rotund bartender who was giving me a dirty look.

"Are you sure you're in the right place?" he asked me. I glanced around and guessed this definitely wasn't a state sanctioned liquor distributor but I got the feeling they could accommodate me if they chose to do so.

"I'm not a cop," I offered.

"I wasn't worried about that," he answered in a harsh tone.

"Just give the man a drink, Russell. Money is money, what do you care?" a voice from beside me said.

I looked over and found a young woman sitting next to me, scolding the bartender who was a little slow with my drink.

She couldn't have been more than twenty and she had large dark eyes and long darker hair. Her skin was the color of milk chocolate, her face smooth and fresh with high cheekbones and a narrow chin, full moist lips pouting above it.

The girl was slim; her well proportioned figure fit snuggly into a white dress with red patterns splattered over the surface, bleached and faded into the fabric. It buttoned up the front and she had it undone just enough to reveal more than ample cleavage straining against the material. She was stunning.

"So are you?" she asked.

"Am I what?"

"Are you in the right place?"

Russell sat a shot glass of booze in front of me and I picked it up and toasted her. "If they serve hooch here I must be in the right place."

As I shot back my drink, there was a sudden burn in my throat and the air was sucked out of my lungs, leaving me hacking and coughing as I swallowed the harsh swill down. "What kind of whiskey is this?" I managed to choke out.

"That's genuine South Carolina White Lightning."

"I'm drinking moonshine?"

"They add a little iodine to it if you ask for whiskey."

"Smooth, what do they make it with, gasoline?"

The girl laughed.

I offered to buy her a drink and she accepted, choosing to have the same as me. There's something about a girl who drinks straight moonshine.

"You here with Bowman?" she asked, gesturing toward the man in the black suit.

I shook my head no. "Just a fan of Blind Eye Regis."

"He really is, you know?"

"He really is what?"

"Blind in one eye."

"What's your name?"

"Tabby."

"Nice to meet you, Tabby."

I gave her my name and ordered us another round of drinks, checking on Bowman's table every so often.

"For somebody that's not with him, you sure seem pretty interested in what he's up to."

I gave her my best smile, unable to look away from those mysterious big browns. "I just can't help thinking that he somehow doesn't fit in here with the rest of us."

Tabby laughed. "So do you work for Chilton, or are you just some crazy white boy?"

"Neither," I kind of lied.

"Yeah, right ..."

"You know Bowman well?"

She stopped smiling. "Everybody around here knows Bowman. I don't think anybody knows him real well."

"Do you have any idea what's going on over there?"

"Yeah, I got an idea."

"Why don't you fill me in?"

"Are you sure you don't work for Chilton?"

I ordered us two more shots. From my breast pocket, I pulled out the envelope Chilton had given me. Ten dollars I placed on the bar to cover our drinks, another twenty I handed to Tabby. "Let's just say I'm a neutral and interested party."

Tabby rolled the twenty and slid it into the deep space between her breasts, pushing it down until it disappeared from view. She gave me a playful, flirty smile as she did, noticing where my eyes were locked the whole time.

"Bowman runs muscle for Old Man Chilton. Everybody in these parts knows Bowman, Chilton not so much. The guy he's talking with is named Hank Reynolds. Hank's father owns a farm not too far from here, been there all his life. I suspect the Reynolds family has worked that farm for three generations or more.

"Right now Hank Reynolds is trying to talk Chet Bowman out of taking his family's farm away. Well, talking Bowman out of helping Chilton take his farm away, anyhow."

"Ouch ..."

"That's the way things work in these parts, Frankie."

"Why does Chilton want to take his family's farm?"

"I suspect he doesn't think he owns enough land around here."

"How did this all happen?"

"The same way it always happens. Old Man Chilton owns the farm supply store. When a farmer needs something he has to go to Chilton."

"The company store."

"Yeah, but around these parts there's some hard times. Sometimes there ain't no money to pay for seed or equipment, sometimes food. Old Man Chilton is only too happy to give these farmers anything they need on credit. Some of these families have been on Chilton's tab for near ten years."

"And when they hit a certain number, Chilton demands payment," I added, figuring out the scam.

"If you ain't got the money, Old Man Chilton takes your farm. I expect it's how he got most of what he's got around here."

"How do you know about this stuff?"

Tabby smiled big, but there was something sad and empty in her smile. "I seen it first hand, Frankie. Old Man Chilton took my family's farm near about four years ago. It all but killed my daddy. What part it didn't the booze took care of. He's been gone almost two years now."

I looked back over at Bowman and Hank Reynolds. Bowman sat stiff with his arms crossed, staring blankly at the younger man as he pleaded and argued.

"The cold-hearted bastard."

"Which one?"

"You ever come across a guy who works for Chilton named Morgan, Tucker Morgan?"

"Yeah, I met him before. He's a bean counter for Chilton. He's as bad as the rest of them. He's the one that figures out how to do it all legal."

Bowman stood up. Hank Reynolds began to get up too, but Bowman pushed him back into his chair. He pointed a finger at the younger man's head and said something to him. It didn't look very friendly. It looked kind of like a threat.

I turned back to Tabby as Bowman came walking by the bar on his way out the door. She had her elbow on the bar and her hand under her chin, supporting the weight of her head in her palm. She was as cute as a damned button and was giving me a curious look.

"You're a strange bird."

"Let me know when he's out the front door."

"You some kind of cop?"

"Not hardly."

"And you don't work for Chilton?"

I shrugged my shoulders and shook my head.

"So what's the interest in Bowman?"

"I'm a friend of Chilton's son. There's some funny stuff going on and I'm trying to get to the bottom of it."

"You're a strange bird and a crazy white boy."

"Thanks."

"He's gone."

"I've got to run, Tabby."

"You going to come back and see me sometime?"

I looked into those pretty brown eyes, that soft delicate face, that charming smile. "I might just do that."

I picked up my fedora and sat it on my noggin, giving Tabby a nod goodbye, and I turned and rushed out the front door.

As I mentioned earlier, I'm really not very good at this whole detective gig. I'm kind of winging my way through it and making it up as I go. I guess that explains what happened next.

I walked out of Mack's Dive like I was on top of the world, cocky and confident. Energized by the smile of a pretty dame and the excitement of being smack dab in the middle of a murder investigation, a first rate detective case.

Darkness had just set in as I stepped out the door and my eyes went immediately to where the blue sedan was parked. My mind had just registered the car was still there when a sharp pain struck me in the gut, knocking the wind out of me and doubling me over.

Chet Bowman straightened me back up and gave me two more jabs to the stomach, then pushed me back and leaned me against the building. I was gasping for air, heaving futilely, unable to get any oxygen to my lungs.

"Why are you following me?" he asked in a sharp tone, his raspy voice like gravel in my ears. I tried to answer but nothing came out.

He took hold of my throat and slammed me into the wall. I was still wheezing, black spots bouncing around in my eyes and water rolling out the corners. All I could do was hold my hands up in an effort to make him stop and give me a second to catch my breath.

"What's your deal? You're that private dick from up north, Bradley's buddy. You got a problem with me?"

I shook my head no.

"You're working for Mr. Chilton, aren't you? He said he paid you a rather sizable fee. You're supposed to be snooping around about the Tucker business."

I nodded, the air just beginning to return to my lungs.

"I don't know why you're tailing me."

"I … didn't … know who … you were," I snorted between breaths.

"Well, now you do." He gave me another shot to the gut. "If you know what's good for you you'll back off and get back to doing what Mr. Chilton's paying you for. I've got nothing to do with Tucker's murder and you're just wasting your time and Mr. Chilton's money following me around. Not to mention the fact that it really pisses me off."

I nodded again.

"You got no business tailing me. What I do has nothing to do with you. My business is between Mr. Chilton and me, it's none of your concern." Again with a jab to my gut.

Now I was getting angry. Lack of oxygen to the brain may have contributed to my bad decision making but I was already getting my ass kicked so what did I have to lose?

Chet Bowman was older than me but he was bigger and he looked a lot rougher around the edges. The one thing I had going for me was I don't fight fair.

Catching whatever breath I could, I scrounged up all the energy I had in me and jerked my knee up into his crotch with all the force I could muster. At the same time, I lunged my face forward, catching him with a head butt to the bridge of the nose as he lurched downward. In an instant he was doubled over, the back of his head exposed and I elbowed him in the sweet spot on the rear of his cranium. He went tumbling down to the ground, his nose broken and bloody, his eyes glazed over. I guess I caught him off guard.

I looked up and down the busy street. People had slowed and stopped to watch the action but nobody looked particularly concerned about our fight, and no one was making any move to come between us.

Bowman was beginning to moan and I had a chance to catch my breath. He didn't look so tough anymore, lying on the ground holding his nuts, blood splattered across his face.

"It's kind of rude to ask somebody a question and punch him

in the gut before he has a chance to answer," I said as I gave him a sharp kick to the side. "And as far as how I do my job, it's none of your damned business.

"I'm not some South Carolina dirt farmer. You might want to consider that the next time you decide to put your paws on me." I squatted down beside him. "It's my turn to ask the questions."

Bowman let out a moan.

"How long you been working for the old man?"

"Twenty years," he grunted.

"You take care of his dirty work, do you? Kick people out of their homes, collect money, that sort of thing?"

He didn't answer.

"How about Michael Tate, did you take care of that problem for him too?"

His eyes got wide for a second like I had hit a nerve or reminded him of something that he hadn't thought about in some time.

"Is everything ok out here?" Tabby said as she came out of the bar and stood over us.

"Everything is honky-dory," I assured her. "Me and my buddy Chet were just having a little chit chat." I looked back down at Bowman. "You might want to get that nose looked at."

I stood back up and winked at Tabby. She seemed to be enjoying the show. "Where can I get a cab?" I asked her.

"Crazy white boy," she sighed, grinning from ear to ear.

Chapter Nineteen

I got back to the Ocean Forest with just enough time to jump into my penguin suit and head back down for dinner. My leg was killing me, my forehead throbbing and my chin was aching where Charlie Jackson punched me earlier. On top of all that, my neck and shoulders were stinging with sunburn. I was a real mess.

By the time I got downstairs everyone was seated for dinner and waiting to be served. This one was something called a rehearsal dinner, an intimate little gathering for three hundred close friends. Earlier in the evening, the bridal party had done a run through of the big event, practice for the looming nuptials. This was the post practice celebration, I suppose.

I found my spot at a small table toward the center of the room. The bridal party sat at the head of the hall at a long table with each of them facing back out at the rest of us, scattered about at smaller round ones. This time I didn't get a chance to have Bradley fix my seating arrangement so instead of sitting with Katherine I ended up with a bunch of strangers discussing Castilians, vacation mansions and the fine art of yachting. Katherine ended up at a table up toward the front. I caught her glancing my way a few times during dinner.

The meal itself was right on par with the first one I'd had at the Ocean Forest. It was one of the great dining experiences of my life, Duck L'Orange served with Shrimp Scampi and fresh asparagus, Chocolate Mousse for desert. I scarfed it down like I hadn't eaten in three days.

After dinner we all made our way out the back of the hotel and down the covered staircase. From there we turned right and walked the fifty yards or so to the open air amphitheater that sat alongside of the hotel. It was a glamorous set up with seating for a hundred people, a large stage for the band and huge dance floor where couples could strut cheek to cheek under the stars.

Tonight it was a local orchestra out of Charleston but I was told that plenty of big names had played there over the years, Tommy Dorsey, Glen Miller and such. As Myrtle Beach was pretty much the half way point between New York and Miami, many big time acts used it as a stopover when touring south, exchanging entertainment for room and board.

We'd had a string quartet entertain us through dinner but now that the plates were being cleared and people were moving outside we were getting a mix of waltzes and swing music, something for the old and the young.

I made my way to the outside bar and ordered a shot. I was standing off to the side by myself but I wouldn't remain alone for long. Gilbert Fleming came walking over and I got the feeling that he'd been looking for me awhile.

"What's the idea, sending me down the river to the cops like that?" he asked, all angry and agitated.

"I was just weeding out the bullshit, nothing personal."

"Yeah, well, if you had a question you could have come to me instead of selling me out to the sheriff and his men."

"I was just trying to get to the truth."

"I've got a good mind to pop you one after what you did to me."

"Get in line," I said.

"It looks like somebody beat me to the punch, literally," he chuckled, staring at the purple welt on my forehead and the bruise on my chin. "For the record ..." he continued, "I didn't kill Tucker Morgan. I never laid a hand on him."

"I never said you did."

"Well, you might as well have, the way you were going on."

"I was just trying to get the straight story."

"Maybe the straight story isn't anybody's business."

"When there's a murder involved it becomes everybody's business."

"You don't know from nothing. I had my reasons for holding back from the cops."

"Yeah, I'm guessing trying to stay out of jail is near the top of that list."

"Maybe I've got something in the works and I don't want it to come unraveled before the deal goes down, ever think of that?"

"What kind of deal?"

Gilbert hesitated. "I'm not at liberty to say at this time but let's just say that it's a very delicate time right now. After this weekend things will be less fragile."

"If you're not careful, after this weekend, you could be sitting in Sing-Sing."

"That's not funny."

"It wasn't meant to be."

"What gives with you? Bradley said you were OK but you've been all over me since you got here."

"Don't you mean since Tucker Morgan was murdered?"

"I told you, I didn't have anything to do with that."

"What were you two arguing about that night?"

"We've already played this song. He was going to go to my father with —"

"With the news that his son was a scoundrel, a fact he already knows," I cut in. "I've heard the song but it just doesn't play on my Victrola."

"Maybe it's time to upgrade to a new phonograph player."

"Maybe it's time to stop playing games and come clean. What were you two really arguing about?"

Gilbert said nothing.

"Did it have something to do with this sensitive deal you have working? Was Tucker Morgan in danger of screwing it up for you?"

His eyes got wide but still he said nothing.

"Be that way. Keep it to yourself. Take it all the way to the hoosegow with you, for all I care."

"You don't really think I killed Tucker, do you?" He seemed sincere and concerned.

"I don't know what to think. All I know is most everybody around here has some kind of skeleton floating around their closet. My guess is one of these skeletons led to the murder of Tucker Morgan."

"It wasn't my skeleton."

"So you say."

"Ask Bradley about me. He'll tell you. Bradley knows I'm on the up and up. If he didn't there's no way he would ..." He stopped short.

"He would what?"

Gilbert shrugged and paused, like he was trying to come up with something, like he had with the sheriff earlier. He wasn't a very good liar.

"There's no way he would marry into my family," he tried but I wasn't buying it. It wasn't what he was going to say.

"Yeah, that makes sense. Why would a guy marry a beautiful, intelligent and sweet girl like Lucy if they knew she had a lying scoundrel for a brother?"

"What do you know?"

"You own a gun, Gilbert?"

His face went a little pale. "Sure, who doesn't? That doesn't make me a murderer."

"Did you bring that gun with you on this little getaway?"

Gilbert didn't answer.

"I'm guessing you did. Guys like you love carrying guns. Makes you feel like Edward G. Robinson, doesn't it?"

He tried to explain to me that he'd left his gun at home but the way he was stuttering and stammering through it gave me the feeling he might be lying. That and the fact his lips were moving.

"I think I've had enough of your tall tales for one day. If you'll excuse me ...".

I walked off, leaving Gilbert Fleming gasping for another response but it was a long time coming and I didn't stick around to catch the next batch of lies.

Across the way, I spotted Katherine in a small group of people, chatting and laughing. She didn't see me approach, and I reached over and grabbed her hand, pulling her away from the crowd.

"Dance?" I asked, but I had her out on the dance floor before she had time to answer.

"That was rude. I was in the middle of a conversation."

"You look beautiful," I said, ignoring her protests.

She did. She was wearing a long lavender gown that hung on spaghetti shoulder straps with a slit up the left side. Her hair was straight and hanging down her back, a golden mane of perfection that framed her flawless face. To top it all off, she smelled like rose pedals.

"Thank you," she answered through red painted lips. "You look like you were in a boxing tournament."

"I ran into a door jamb."

"How did the door jamb look?"

I pulled her in close and pressed my face against hers, leading her into the slow dance across the center of the floor, memorizing what she felt like snuggled in against me and in my arms.

The back of her dress was open and my right hand was resting on her bare lower back, just above her hips, my left holding her right hand at shoulder level. She was soft and smooth and warm in my arms. I closed my eyes and concentrated on every part of her that was touching me, soaking in as much of her as I could get.

As far as dancers go, I'm just about good enough not to step on a girl's foot or break her ankle. I'm not going to win any foxtrot contests but I have enough moves to get by. On that night, I felt like Fred Astaire gliding across the floor with Ginger Rogers. It was like I had been dancing with Katherine all my life.

I pulled my head back and looked into her silky brown eyes. "You know, if you and I are going to be friends like I'd like to be, you're going to have to be straight with me."

"I thought we *were* friends," she purred.

"I just had a little talk with Gilbert."

"Is he the one that did a number on your face?"

"No, but I'm guessing he wishes he was."

"Oh, he's harmless."

"What's the deal with him and Bradley? Do they have something in the works?"

Katherine looked a little dumbstruck. "I wouldn't know anything about that. Neither of them would discuss such things with me."

"There's something off kilter about that Gilbert. Things just don't add up."

"Gilbert is just ...Gilbert."

"Gilbert is also the lead suspect in a murder case."

She giggled. "Gilbert is not a murderer."

"How can you be so sure?"

"I just know is all."

"Well, he's in quite a pickle either way."

"He's a lot of things and not many of them good, but he's not a killer."

"Tell me more about the Flemings. How did they lose their money? Who was the business partner that screwed Herbert over?"

"I wouldn't know anything about that; it was a little before my time. I was just a child when most of that happened."

"You must know something."

"Well ..." She paused, looking around, hesitating while deciding whether or not she should go further. "I really shouldn't say anything. It's not my place, and I only know from things I've heard ..."

"With an intro like that you can't stop now."

Katherine leaned her head into my shoulder and turned into my neck, talking softly, almost whispering. Her words were quiet and cautious and I could feel her warm breath on my throat with every one she uttered.

"I guess it was a few years ago, but he and Mr. Chilton had a big falling out. It really wasn't until Lucy and Bradley got engaged they even began talking again."

"A falling out? That sounds juicy."

"Yeah."

"What was it over?"

"As I heard it, Herbert Fleming was already in a financial bind. He had been struggling to recover from some bad business deals

135

for years. Apparently he owned a track of land just to the south of Myrtle Beach, undeveloped, not very valuable. Mr. Chilton offered to buy it. He gave him what was considered fair market value."

"That doesn't sound too bad." I said.

"Yeah, until six months later when Mr. Chilton turned around and sold it to the Government for five times what he paid. It was part of the land they built the Army Air Base on. "

"So Herbert Fleming had a reason to hold a grudge."

"He swore up and down that Chilton knew about the Army Air Field deal when he bought the land. He figures he was swindled by Chilton."

"I'm guessing Tucker Morgan had a hand in that deal too."

"Probably."

"That presents motive for Herbert Fleming, Gilbert too for that matter."

"I wouldn't know about all that. I don't see either one of them killing anyone. "

"That's usually the way it works. Nobody is a killer until they go out and kill somebody," I explained. "What about Bradley? Did he have anything to do with the army base deal?"

Katherine lifted her head and looked at me funny. "Heavens no, Bradley was still in school."

"From everything I'm hearing Old Man Chilton is a first class son of a bitch."

"That seems to be the consensus."

"I get the sense Bradley thinks so."

"You would have to ask Bradley about that."

"Let's talk about Bradley."

"What is there to talk about?"

"You and him for starters."

She shifted uneasily in my arms. "It was a long time ago. It's hardly worth mentioning."

"It wasn't that long ago."

"We were a couple and now we're not. That's all there is to it."

"Why did he break it off?"

"He fell in love with Lucy." She said it sharp and stiff, no emotion in her voice.

"You still have feelings for him."

"Can't we talk about something else?"

"From where I'm standing it looks like you're carrying a pretty big torch around."

"Don't be silly."

"If I didn't know any better I'd say he's got one with your name on it too."

"Then you don't know any better."

"What's the deal with you two? What were you doing in his hotel room?"

"I don't know what you're talking about."

"You two are pretty chummy for a couple of exs."

Katherine stopped dancing and dropped her arms to her sides. She was looking up at me with a look somewhere between hurt and anger. "Are you accusing me of something?"

"I'm just trying to get the low down."

"If you have something to say, just say it."

"Ok, I think you're still in love with Bradley. I think he's still in love with you too. I think there's still something between the two of you. What I can't figure is why he broke it off in the first place."

Katherine had tears welling in her eyes. "You don't know what you're talking about."

"Why did he get so jealous on the beach when you kissed me?"

"You would have to ask him about that."

"As I remember, you were pretty short with him as well."

"I was not."

"What's going on between the two of you?"

She shoved me back with two hands, barely budging me, and stormed off. Across the dance floor and toward the ocean, she walked away, down the steps that led off into the darkness.

I gave it a few moments before I followed.

The ocean was calm, small waves rolling in off her surface and dissipating into the shoreline, evaporating into the sand. The moon wasn't whole but it was bright enough to illuminate the scene in bluish light. It looked like a scene painted on canvas, all blues and purples, the occasional black thrown in for effect.

I trudged out into the sand and worked my way south, moving away from the hotel and passing a couple of stray party goers as I went. Off in the distance I caught sight of something in the sand dunes. I could make out the outline of blonde hair blowing back in the ocean breeze.

She didn't acknowledge me as I approached. She sat curled up with her knees in her face and her arms wrapped around her legs, her head hanging low. I got the impression she was crying.

Settling into the sand beside her, I snuggled in against her, leaning into her side. "I didn't mean to hurt your feelings."

Katherine didn't answer.

"Look, maybe I came off a little harsh but I care about you. I can't stand seeing you treated this way. I can't stand to see what you're doing to yourself."

She looked up at me and I could see the tears running down her face. The makeup around her eyes was smudged a little and the moonlight gave her face a pale silver glow, ghostly and somber.

"I can't stomach what he's doing to you."

"You don't understand."

"Maybe I do understand. Bradley wants it all. He wants the cozy little homemaker and the home in the country, the white picket fence and a house full of rug rats. He also wants you."

"It's not like that."

"It's not? Then what's it like?"

Katherine didn't answer.

"I love Bradley as much as anybody. Hell, I owe him my life, but it's not right what he's doing. He's getting greedy. He wants the best of all worlds. He wants to be rich and successful and stick it to his father, and he wants the perfect little wife with the girl of his dreams on the side. Maybe he's more like the old man than he thinks."

"Bradley's doing what he has to do."

"Is he? What about you? What about what he's putting you through? Does he know what it's like for you to sit back and watch him with Lucy? Does he have any idea what you go through every time you have to watch him put his arms around her, every time he kisses her? Does he have any idea what it's going to be like for you when you have to sit back and watch him take his vows?"

The tears were coming pretty good by now. I reached up and took her chin in my finger tips, turning her head toward me, fixing her eyes on mine and leaning in close to her.

"You're too good for this. You deserve better."

"You just don't get it."

"No, you don't get it, Katherine. Any guy that would put you through this isn't worth your time. You should be with a guy who treats you like gold, like the sun revolves around you.

"You're special, Katherine. I knew it the first time I laid eyes on you. You're not like Lucy or any other girl. You're beautiful and intelligent and funny and any guy in the world would be lucky for the privilege of worshipping you.

"You should be with a guy that sees that. You should be with a guy who gets how precious you are, not a guy who strings you along and treats you like this."

"A guy like you?" she asked and her voice was soft and trembling, high pitched and vulnerable like a little girl's.

I slid my hand around to the back of her head, weaving my fingers into her hair and I pulled her toward me, planting a kiss on her lips. It wasn't the gentle, tender kiss like the day on the beach. This kiss was hard and passionate, forceful and deadly serious.

She responded by tilting her head to the side and kissing me back, matching my fury. Both of us lost in a haze of lust, passion and blind fervor with the ocean serving as the soundtrack of the night.

Katherine let herself fall backwards into the dunes and I followed on top of her, wrapping myself around her. I had my face in her neck, kissing her throat and ears, devouring her soft flesh with my lips, ignoring the fact that my head was sticking in the sand.

My left hand was wedged in between her back and the ground and I began exploring her body with my right, running it across the surface of her, pawing at her delicious curves, completely out of control. My mind was a frenzy of senses and images bouncing around inside of my skull, barely comprehensible.

I reached up to her left shoulder and peeled the thin strap

away from her skin, pushing it down her body.

"I can't ..." she moaned lightly but I didn't believe her or chose to ignore her. Her eyes were closed and she was panting quietly, her lips slightly parted. I kissed them again, nibbling gently on the bottom lip as I did.

Katherine reached up across her body and pulled at the right shoulder strap of her dress, bringing it down and working her arm out of it. Together, without a word, we pulled and tugged at the long gown, pushing it down her body, guiding it across her torso, past her hips and the length of her long legs until it lay in a pile by her feet. She was left in only a brassiere and panties.

She hesitated for a moment before raising her upper body slightly and reaching behind her back, unfastening the garment. It fell limp across her chest and I reached over and pulled it off, tossing it to the side.

Digging her heels into the sand, she lifted her bottom into the air and placed her thumbs inside the band of her panties, peeling them down and pushing them away from her hips. I took them from there and scooted them down her legs as she lifted one foot out of them and I left them dangling off her left ankle. She was completely naked.

I stopped for a second, glancing over her. She was lying in the sand, her right arm across her chest, covering her nudity, her body rising and falling with deep silent breaths. Her hair was spread out across the ground in total disarray and there was a lost look across her stunning face.

She was the most beautiful thing I had ever seen and the sight of the moonlight dancing off her skin nearly took my breath away. I loosened my tie and began to unbutton my shirt.

Making love to Katherine Mathews in the sand was nothing short of a benchmark moment in my life. It's one of those images a guy can hang on to forever, something to keep you warm on those long winter nights.

We dressed in silence, her avoiding my gaze, me studying every motion she made, watching as she zipped, fastened and pulled herself back to wholeness. When she was finished she walked up to me, barefoot in the sand and carrying her shoes.

Katherine wiped the hair from her face and held it aside,

trying to keep it from whipping back in the wind, looking up at me and biting down slightly on her lip. She looked out of place in the long gown, tousled and uncombed, no longer the image of elegance and sophistication she had been at the party. Now she was something different, something smaller and exposed, something more lovely than I had ever imagined.

I stepped forward and took her in my arms, kissing her softly on the lips. If I could have thought of any words I would have said them, but instead I stood there holding her, wondering what was going on behind those mysterious eyes.

Katherine took my hand and guided me out of the dunes and back to the beach. We walked hand in hand up the coast, neither of us saying a word, her leaning in on my shoulder as we went.

The night seemed brighter than before, the Atlantic even calmer, her surface like glass and stretching out into infinity. The old gal seemed to be whispering to me, rolling her message to me in her waves, sparkling it across the top of her depths in some kind of moonlit Morse Code.

I was too dumb to get her meaning, my skull too thick to catch what she was trying to tell me, but looking out over her, with Katherine by my side, I felt myself let go of some of the hatred I had for her. I felt myself begin to forgive her for what she had taken from me on that beach two years before.

We stopped short of the Ocean Forest and kissed again, still far enough away not to be seen by any of the guests, our last private moment before returning to the world.

I don't know what I was expecting. Maybe I wanted her to profess her love for me and promise that we would always be together. Maybe I wanted one of those sappy love scenes from the movies, the kind you know lead to the happy ending everybody came to see. It didn't go down like that.

"I'm sorry," Katherine said in a soft sigh, kissing me on the side of my face. "This was a mistake."

She turned and trotted off, making her way around the back of the hotel and heading for the side entrance, avoiding the party completely. I was left stunned and standing in the sand, trying to register what she had said to me.

I don't know how long I stood there.

141

Chapter Twenty

I learned the hard way that making love on the beach had its drawbacks, the main one being the sand. It tends to get into places sand wasn't meant to be. It's a lot like wearing sandpaper underpants and it made the walk back up to the hotel uncomfortable, to say the least.

I strolled up the steps and back into the amphitheater. The party was going strong and the band was playing a Benny Goodman number. I decided a drink was in order. At the bar I stood off to the side drinking my whiskey and chasing it with water. I was working on my third one when Bradley made his way over.

"Hey there, stranger, where have you been hiding?"

"I took a little walk on the beach," I told him.

"The beach, I thought you hated the beach?"

"It's beginning to grow on me."

I finished off my shot and took a deep breath. It was time Bradley and I had a little talk. "Does Lucy suspect anything?"

He smiled a weird smile, his eyes dancing around for a moment. "Does she suspect what?"

"Does she suspect you and Katherine?"

Bradley laughed. "She knows all about me and Katherine. It's not like it was a big secret."

"I know she knows about your past but does she suspect anything is going on now?"

"Are you drunk?"

"You need to cut her loose. It's not fair to Katherine or Lucy."

"Look, Frankie, I know you've taken a shining to Katherine but …"

"Let her go, Bradley."

He looked around nervously and took a drink from his Martini glass. "What did she tell you?"

"She didn't tell me anything. She didn't have to."

"This is ridiculous."

"What is this all about? If you wanted to be with Katherine you could have. You had her. Why the games? Why are you marrying Lucy?"

"I happen to be very much in love with Lucy."

"Does this have anything to do with your father, marrying the daughter of his rival? Are you looking to get back at your old man?"

"My father and Herbert Fleming are old and dear friends, not rivals."

"They were old and dear friends until your old man bought that chunk of land from him and turned around and sold it to the government so they could build their army air field. That's not the kind of thing old and dear friends do to each other. "

"Who told you about that?"

"What difference does it make, it's true."

"I suppose it is. My father's a businessman."

"A pretty ruthless one, from what I hear."

"That's my father, it's not me."

"Do you have something in the works involving Gilbert?"

"I plan to become his brother-in-law, if that's what you mean."

"No big business deal?"

"What's with the third degree?"

"I'm just trying to figure out what's going on around here."

"Nothing is going on. All this Tucker Morgan business is making you paranoid. If there's something you want to know just ask me. Don't go around listening to the gossip of others."

I paused for a second, wishing I had another shot of whiskey and shifted my weight on my leg, trying to dislodge some unwanted grit from a secret place without being too obvious. "Do you remember much about your mother before her ... affliction?"

"Of course I do. What kind of question is that?"

"Do you know anything about how she ended up in the condition she is now?"

Bradley's face turned red and the niceness drained out of it. "Maybe we should put a stop to this conversation before one of us says something we'll regret."

"You said I could ask anything I wanted."

"I think you should go sleep it off, Frankie. The booze is hampering your good judgment." The smile returned to his face, forced as it was. "Get a good night's sleep, tomorrow we're off to the racetrack. It's my last day as a single man and I'm feeling like a little debauchery."

"That's pretty debaucherous."

"We can talk more when you're sober."

"I'm sober now."

"You've had too much to drink and you're on the verge of making a jackass of yourself. I suggest you go and retire for the evening."

"Maybe I'm not tired."

"Maybe you should go to bed anyway."

"What are you hiding?"

"This isn't the time or the place."

"When is the time and place," I said, my voice louder than I had meant. "When do I get some straight answers from you?"

People were beginning to stop and take notice. I was creating a scene.

"What's wrong, Bradley? Are you afraid I might reveal the skeletons in your closet? You needn't worry." I looked around at the people staring at me. "If there's one thing I've learned since I got here it's that everyone around this dump has skeletons in their closet. There are enough skeletons in this place to fill a cemetery."

"Go to bed, Frankie."

I turned and stumbled past the bar, through the crowd and out into the night, making my way toward the hotel entrance, ignoring the stares and looks of disgust I was getting from the other guests. Bradley had been right about one thing, I was drunk. I needed to get to bed and clear my head with a solid eight hours of shut eye.

In the lobby, as I was on my way to the elevator, Sheriff Talbert was standing at the front desk talking to the hotel manager as I came walking by. He was giving me the hairy eyeball as I approached.

"What happened to your face?"

"A water polo accident."

"It might interest you to know we got the ballistics report back. Tucker Morgan was done in with a .38 caliber."

"Pretty common gun."

"You own a gun?"

"Yeah, I own one."

"Mind if I take a look at it?"

"It's back up in Baltimore. Give me a minute and I'll run home and get it. "

"What kind of gun is it, if you don't mind me asking?"

"I'm more of a .45 kind of girl," I answered. "So, what, am I a suspect now?"

"As far as I'm concerned, everybody is a suspect."

"What happened to Gilbert Fleming?"

"It turns out Gilbert Fleming has an alibi. He was in a little bar not far from here with a certain young lady."

"What time was that?"

"Right about the time Tucker Morgan was getting himself dead."

"And you're sure he's telling the truth?"

"There were witnesses."

"Well, that's that then."

"It's a funny thing about that bar. Earlier today some Yankee was in there asking a lot of questions. He ended up getting into it with one of the locals, got himself socked in the jaw."

"You know how those Yankees are."

"The guy he was mixing it up with was a fellow by the name

145

of Jackson. It turns out he's married to a girl who works in the same office as your buddy, a girl named Dorothy."

"Why, Sheriff, it sounds like you've been out doing some first rate detective work."

"There's more," he said with a shit-eating grin. "Rumor has it this Dorothy girl was pretty friendly with Tucker Morgan. Some people are wondering exactly how friendly her relationship with Morgan was."

"I'm impressed, Sheriff. You're a regular Sherlock Holmes."

"The only thing I can't figure out is what this Yankee fellow was doing snooping around."

"Maybe he was lost, looking to get directions."

"He was lost all right. I've got a feeling he doesn't realize just how lost he is."

"If I bump into him I'll try to put him on the right track."

"You do that."

I wandered off to the elevator. Inside the cramped little box, Freckle Face was pissing me off, just standing there and doing his job. By the time we got to my floor, I was fuming mad.

"Have a nice night, sir," he said as I got off. He didn't even have the attitude this time.

"Shut the hell up." I didn't like the way he said it.

Chapter Twenty-One

Once again, I awoke to the phone ringing. This time I felt a little better. I had another hangover but this one was nothing compared to the previous day, barely registering on the 'I feel crummy' scale.

I glanced at my wristwatch. It was almost eleven.

"Yeah?" I said into the receiver.

"I've been calling you all morning. You missed breakfast." There is a God.

"I decided to sleep in."

"Well, get up," Bradley continued. There was no animosity in his voice. "We're leaving for the track in twenty minutes."

"I'll be right down."

By the time I got dressed and downstairs the entire gang was gathered in the lobby. Most of the players were there. Alfred Chilton and Herbert Fleming were both dressed in tweed suits, Bradley and Gilbert in slacks and sweaters. Mrs. Chilton was wearing a dress almost identical to the one she had worn the previous day except this one was purple. Mrs. Fleming had decided to go with a tan dress with large brown lapels.

Lucy was in a light cotton summer dress, white and clingy. Katherine's was a pale blue, frilly and domestic looking, her hair pulled back in a ponytail. All the women were wearing bonnets.

I was in my usual grey wool suit.

Bradley was the first to approach me. He patted me on the shoulder. "How are you feeling today? You were in pretty rare form last night."

"I'm fine," I answered, half expecting him to punch me in the face.

"It's all good," he said, patting me again. "No harm done."

"We should be going," the older Chilton said. "I don't want to miss the first race."

There were three cars waiting out front for us. The Flemings drove in one car, the Chiltons drove in another, I went with Bradley, Lucy, Gilbert and Katherine in the last. I was wedged in the back seat between Gilbert and Katherine. She was doing her best not to look at me as we climbed in. She didn't get any friendlier as we took off for the racetrack.

We pulled down the circular driveway in front of the Ocean Forest and out onto the main road, making a left and heading toward Myrtle Beach.

The Washington Park Race Track sat on the corner of Oak Street and 21st Avenue, along a road that ran through the middle of town with little else on it. Past the racetrack the road pretty much dead ended into the wilderness.

The racetrack itself was a horse track that specialized in harness races. It was a nice enough place, surrounded by a white vertical board fence, inside was a half mile oval track with seating all around. There wasn't a bad seat in the house.

It was sectioned off in different degrees of money. There was an infield where the regular folks hung, picnicking and hanging out, enjoying an afternoon with the family. There was a grandstand where the next level of customers gathered, young couples enjoying the day out, the middle class, the hard core gamblers. We were up in the private boxes, large open booths under the overhang roof reserved for the wealthier patrons of the track. There was a spread of food and a bartender on duty.

For lunch we were having a local dish called Shrimp and Grits. It wasn't half bad, grits and all.

After a quick study of the local racing form, the ladies settled in and the men, minus Herbert Fleming who wasn't much of a gambler, went down to place bets on the first race. I put five dollars on a horse called Lap of Luxury.

While we were walking back I saw a familiar, albeit bandaged, face coming our way. Chet Bowman gave me a dirty look as he approached but didn't say a word to me. There was a strip of medical tape across the bridge of his swollen nose and both his eyes were black. He took Chilton off to the side and the rest of us continued on to the box.

I took a seat next to Katherine but she was still doing a pretty good job of ignoring me, too wrapped up in conversation with the ladies to pay me any attention. Mostly they talked about local happenings and upcoming social engagements. When the conversation turned to the Tucker Morgan murder, even the men began paying attention.

"From what I hear, the police are investigating Dorothy Jackson's husband regarding Tucker's death," Lydia Fleming said.

"I heard something about that," Lucy added. "They say she was seeing Tucker on the side. Can you imagine?"

I threw in my two cents. "It's all hearsay for now."

"I understand Charlie Jackson has quite the temper," Lucy continued. "You're the detective but jealousy is a quite common motive for murder, isn't it, Frankie?"

"It's in the top five."

"What would you say is the number one?"

"Lucy, don't be so morbid," her mother scolded.

"There's nothing morbid about it. I'm simply curious, is all. What would you say, Frankie, is the most common motive for murder?"

I lit a smoke. "Well, jealousy is right up there but I'd have to go with greed."

"So, you think more people are killed over money than love?"

"If you have enough money you can always find love."

"Spoken like a man who's never had money," Gilbert cut in with a chuckle. "No offense."

"None taken," I said. "Sometimes they go hand in hand but yes, I'd say greed is the most popular."

"How would they go hand in hand?" Lucy asked.

"Well, maybe a guy has it bad for a girl but he doesn't have the financial clout to make it work. Maybe a guy has to resort to drastic measures to keep the girl of his dreams. Some girls are looking for a little more out of life and love isn't enough."

"Some guys too," Gilbert joked.

"What do you think, Katherine?" Lucy asked.

Katherine looked up a little stunned, like she had only been half paying attention to the conversation, lost in her own thoughts. "I'm afraid I wouldn't know."

"Oh please, don't be a fuddy-duddy, you must have an opinion."

Taking a sip from her glass of lemonade, Katherine cocked her head to the side and thought about it for a second. When she answered, she was looking directly at Lucy. "I suppose there isn't much I wouldn't do for love but I don't think I could kill anyone."

Lucy was staring back at Katherine with a whimsical smile but a serious look in her eyes. "So, what you're saying is, you would do practically anything in the name of love, short of murder."

"Yes." There was no hesitation in her answer.

"Well, I guess that's good to know, isn't it?"

I was pulled away from the discussion by a tap on my shoulder and I looked up to find Alfred Chilton hovering over me. "May I have a word with you?"

"Certainly," I said, getting up and following him out of the box. He took me to a secluded area under the grandstand and I could tell by the look on his face there was something bothering him. I had a pretty good hunch what it was.

"What's the meaning of attacking my man Bowman?"

"Is that what he told you?"

"I saw what you did to the man's face."

"After four or five punches in the gut I tend to get annoyed."

"Why were you following him in the first place?"

"I didn't even know who he was."

"You could have asked."

"Where's the sport in that?"

"I am not paying you to follow and harass my people."

"No, you're paying me to look out for your people and keep

150

them out of this messy ordeal. I can't very well do that if I don't know what they're up to."

"I can assure you that Chet Bowman has nothing to do with any of this. He's a very loyal employee who has been in my service for many years," the old man said in an agitated voice.

"That sounds an awful lot like Tucker Morgan, doesn't it?"

"Look here. I don't know what kind of people you are used to dealing with where you come from but down here we—"

I cut him off. "I know, you conduct yourselves with a certain amount of decorum, I heard it all before. From where I'm standing, you people are swimming in decorum but decorum isn't going to get to the bottom of this."

"Maybe you misunderstood my instructions."

"Maybe you misunderstood the fact that I'm not interested in your instructions. I'm not one of your flunkies. If you don't like the way I conduct my business fire me." I pulled the envelope he'd given me from my jacket and held it out for him to take. "It's all there, minus a few bucks for drinks and expenses I incurred. You can have it back if you want."

Chilton looked at the envelope and then back at me. He made no move to take it.

"Do you want to tell me about Michael Tate?"

The old man's eyes got wide, like the name came as a cold slap in the face. "Why are you drudging up names from the past, what's that have to do with anything?"

"I don't know yet. Sometimes you just have to throw things into the fan and see where they land."

"Where did you hear that name?"

"A little bird told me."

"No good can from throwing around wild accusations which you know nothing about. A lot of people could get hurt in the process."

"Why don't you tell me about Michael Tate?"

"That matter is none of your concern. It was a very long time ago."

"What happened to him?"

"How should I know? He went back home, I suppose."

"Where was home?"

151

"Georgia or something, what has this to do with anything?"

"Did he leave of his own accord?"

"I don't know what it is you think you know but I suggest you spend less time listening to local gossip and more time concentrating on the job you're being paid to do."

Chilton's face was blood red and I could see the veins protruding from his temples. It was fairly obvious that I'd done a good job getting under the old man's skin. Why stop now?

"How are things with you and Herbert Fleming these days?"

"More gossip?"

"I hear tell you two were on the ropes for awhile, something to do with that US Army Air Field deal."

"I bought a parcel of land from Herbert. I did it out of the goodness of my own heart in an attempt to help a friend in need. Down the road, an opportunity to sell the land presented itself. I did what any good business man would do."

"Yeah, I've heard about some of those good deeds you're so famous for. You're very popular with the local farmers."

"I don't expect you to understand how I conduct my business dealings."

"No, I wouldn't think you would," I replied. "Tell me one thing ... "

"What?"

"That deal with the army air field, how much did Tucker Morgan have to do with that?"

"What does that matter?"

"Just answer the question."

Chilton gave it some thought. "Tucker was my right hand man at the time. He was very involved with all my business matters. He would have had a great deal to do with anything that went through the office."

"What about that deal? How much did he have to do with that one?"

"As I remember, it was his idea to buy the land off of Herbert. I had mentioned that Herbert was looking to sell some assets and Tucker did the research. He was the one who suggested we invest in that particular parcel."

"And six months later, when the government came knocking?"

Chilton thought some more. "It was Tucker who negotiated the deal with the government."

"Let me ask you something else, did Tucker make out on that deal?"

"Well, the firm made a sizable profit on that transaction. He received a significant commission. That is nothing out of the ordinary."

"That's what I thought."

"What are you getting at?"

"I'm just doing my job."

He didn't seem too impressed. The look on his face was similar to that of a guy chewing on tin foil. He shook his head and walked away disgusted.

Back at the box, everyone was enjoying the spectacle of harness racing; the first race had just begun. I took my seat next to Katherine.

"How is my nag doing?" I leaned in and asked her.

She looked back at me with a funny look.

"My horse? Lap of Luxury?"

"Dead last," she answered.

She wasn't kidding. My horse finished about five minutes after the rest of the pack. So much for luxury.

"Can we talk?" I was keeping my voice low enough so only Katherine could hear. No one else seemed to be paying attention.

"Not now," she whispered back.

"I'd rather not do this here."

Katherine looked around nervously, maybe imagining the scene I might cause.

"Ok."

We stood and excused ourselves under the pretense we were going for a walk, Katherine showing me around. Nobody seemed concerned. Bradley looked our way for a moment but turned his attentions back to the track without a word. I wondered if it was all for show.

"What is it?" she asked as we made our way around the back of the grandstand.

"You're a little cold today, don't you think?"

"I don't know what you want me to say."

153

"I want you to tell me what's going on with you."

"There's nothing going on with me. I told you, last night was a mistake."

"As far as mistakes go, I thought it was a pretty spectacular one."

"That's not what I meant."

"What did you mean?"

"Do we have to do this right now?"

I stopped and took her by the arm, turning her around to face me and moving in close.

"Look, I'm not stupid. It's not like I expected you to go all mushy on me after what happened. I realize I'm not in the same league as you're used to, but I didn't expect to get the cold shoulder."

"It's not like that."

"Then what is it like?"

"You just don't understand."

"Make me understand."

She was looking up at me with watery eyes. Her face was drawn and stressed.

"Look, Frankie, you're a great guy but I did a dreadful thing."

"It wasn't that bad, was it?"

She ignored my little joke. "I shouldn't have done what I did."

"There were two of us on that beach, you know."

"I never meant to hurt you."

"Does this have something to do with him?"

She didn't answer.

"He's engaged, he's getting married tomorrow. What do you care what he thinks?"

"That's not it. You can't possibly understand."

"Explain it to me."

"I'm sorry, Frankie, I can't. You just have to believe me and know that I'm truly sorry for putting you in this position."

"What position?"

Katherine leaned up and gave me a soft kiss to the cheek. "Just know that I really truly think the world of you, and no matter what happens I never meant you any harm. I'm very sorry for everything."

"You're not making any sense."

"I know."

"So, that's that?"

She nodded, slow and soft.

"I guess there's not much else to say then. I know how to take a hint."

"I never meant to hurt you. I didn't think it would be this hard."

"Life can be a real bitch sometimes."

"I'm sorry," she repeated, turning and walking away, leaving me alone under the wooden seats.

I could lie and say that it didn't hurt, but it did. It hurt a lot. It was like getting hit in the chest with a javelin.

Don't get me wrong. I never figured to end up riding off into the sunset with a gal like Katherine Mathews. Four days earlier I would have said you were crazy if you had told me she'd even give a mug like me the time of day. Just the same, I really liked being around her. I liked looking at her and I liked the way she smelled, the way she felt when she was pressed in against me. I liked the way she crinkled her nose when she laughed. Most of all, I liked talking to her.

Pretty sappy for a guy like me.

I gave myself about a minute and a half to feel sorry for myself. After that, it was time to move on, time to pull myself together. The best way I knew to do that was to get mad. I figured I had plenty to be mad about. Before heading back, I stopped off at the lounge for a couple of quick belts of bourbon.

By the time I got back the whole gang was off placing bets on the next race. The only one left behind was Herbert Fleming. Mrs. Chilton was there too, but I didn't count her. She was there physically but I got the sense her head was somewhere else.

I sat down beside Mr. Fleming.

"How are you doing, win anything?" I knew damned well he wasn't a betting man.

"I don't gamble."

"Not on horses, anyway."

"What is that supposed to mean?"

"It's just that business is sort of a gamble, isn't it? The buying and selling of real estate? You never really know how it's going to end up."

"This is true."

"Take that army base deal, who knew that would turn out the way it did?"

Herbert shot me a cold look.

"Chilton made out pretty good on that one."

"Yes, he did."

"Tucker Morgan did OK on that one too."

"I wouldn't know."

"But you did know that Morgan was the one who orchestrated that whole thing, didn't you?"

"I had my suspicions."

"It must have really gotten under your collar when that whole thing came out, huh?"

"I was upset, to say the least."

"Did you ever confront Tucker Morgan about it?"

"We had some words. I had a good talking to with Alfred as well."

"I bet you did."

"Who wouldn't?"

"Let me ask you, how long do you hold a grudge over something like that?"

"What are you getting at?"

"I'm just asking, is all. I'm guessing a thing like that could be a thorn in your side for a lot of years."

"I'm not going to lie. I was considerably bitter for some time, but I got over it."

"Did you? Are you sure you never wanted to get back at the people responsible?"

"Are you accusing me of something?"

"Should I be?"

"It's no secret that I had no love lost for either Alfred Chilton or Tucker Morgan. I told them as much. I made no secret of my feelings at the way they conducted the entire affair. That said, when Lucy and Bradley became a couple I felt it was in the best interest of everyone involved to put it all behind us."

"It sounds pretty easy when you say it like that."

"My daughter's welfare is far more important than any feelings I might harbor one way or the other."

"Just the same, it would have felt pretty good to get some payback."

"The bible teaches us to turn the other cheek."

"Yeah, and it says an eye for an eye too."

"What are you getting at?"

"I'm getting at motive. The kind of motive it takes to shoot another man in the face."

"Are you mad? Do you think I killed Tucker Morgan?"

"I'm just having a friendly conversation."

Herbert Fleming stood up, disgust written all over his face. "Young man, no matter how angry I might be at another man I would never resort to the use of violence to resolve a dispute. I do not operate in that manner and I am insulted that you would even suggest such a thing."

"What about Gilbert? He had a stake in this too. That land you sold off was part of his inheritance, wasn't it?"

"Are you accusing my son of murder?"

"He is a bit of a loose cannon. Everyone knows of his wild reputation."

"This conversation is over. I refuse to be subjected to this vile talk any longer."

With that, Herbert Fleming made a hasty exit. I looked over to Harriet Chilton. She looked to be oblivious to me or my conversation with Herbert.

"How are you, Mrs. Chilton?" I asked in a loud voice, as though she were deaf. She cocked her head and shot me a look. It was the kind of look a person has when they're trying to decipher hieroglyphics. "How are you feeling today?"

Still nothing.

"Mrs. Chilton, do you ever hear from Michael Tate these days?"

Her eyes got wide and an eerie expression crossed her face. I couldn't tell if I had hit a nerve or just yanked her out of a benign state of semi-consciousness. I figured I was heading down a dead end road.

Sitting back in my seat, I mulled things over. There was no telling if it had been a good idea to confront Herbert Fleming the way I did, but sometimes you have to poke the beehive with a stick a few times and see which way the swarm comes flying. The tricky part, I knew, was to do it without getting stung.

Chapter Twenty-Two

*T*he rest of the afternoon was weird, to say the least. It was pleasant and entertaining to an extent but I couldn't help feel like I was a bit ostracized by the rest of the group. Of course, there was my deal with Katherine, which made enough sense. Alfred Chilton wasn't one of my biggest fans either. After my encounter with Herbert Fleming, I doubted I'd be getting a Christmas card from him come December.

Gilbert was already opposed to my being around and Lydia Fleming was probably neutral at best. Even Lucy had been at odds with me as late. About the only one who didn't hold a grudge against me was Mrs. Chilton, but I'm not sure she even knew who I was. I'd even had a blow out with my best friend, Bradley, although he didn't show any animosity toward me.

Everyone laughed and joked and followed the day's races, sometimes winning but mostly losing. I, personally, lost twenty-three dollars before it was all over. It was OK, though, as it was Chilton's money.

When the races were finished, we gathered up and set out back to the Ocean Forest. It looked like we were going back the way we came, but Bradley threw a wrench into the works. He decided he and I should take a little ride together. He wanted to show me some of the local sights. It took some finagling but we reworked the seating arrangements so Bradley and I ended up in a car alone.

We got into the Cadillac convertible and he drove me off, away from the beach, turning down a road that looked a lot like the road I had explored alone. We were out in the middle of nowhere when he pulled it off to the side.

"What do you think," he asked.

"Nice," I answered.

Bradley got out of the car and walked across the dirt road. I followed.

"Do you know what this is?" he asked.

"A great place to dump a body?"

"This is the future of Myrtle Beach."

I looked around. It was wetlands and forest, thick and undeveloped. It looked more like the past than the future.

"Frankie, I have a vision. I can see what this place could become."

"Visions are good."

Bradley pointed out to the west. "Over there will be one of the premiere golf courses on the east coast, top of the line, first class, beside it, two adjoining courses, less expensive, affordable to the average Joe.

"Adjacent to that will be a resort with a state of the art complex, shopping, entertainment, amusement park. You name it, we'll have it. In five years this will be the vacation capital of the east coast."

"Impressive."

"This is the direction Myrtle Beach is heading."

"What does Daddy think about all this?"

"My father is narrow-minded. He thinks the future of this town is in industry and agriculture. The future of Myrtle Beach is tourism. There will be a day when millions of people will flock to this area."

"Millions? That's a lot of people."

"This place is a gold mine, Frankie. Once we have easy access to the outside world, there's no telling how big this could be."

"Yeah, if only you could get them to put a highway through here," I said, all smartass and sly.

"You know about that?"

"I've heard things."

"Then you know this is a can't miss deal. This place is going to blow up."

"If your father is so intent on this town being about industry and agriculture, how do you plan on slipping this by him? He's the one with the capital, isn't he?"

"You let me worry about that. I've got everything worked out. I'm going to turn this town into something special, something the entire world will know about. The Ocean Forest is amazing but how many American families can afford to stay there?"

"So now you have your finger on the pulse of the American family, huh?"

"I'm going to offer something for everyone; golf for the grown-ups and movie houses and amusements for the kids, the complete vacation package."

"Sounds good but why are you telling me all this?"

"I'm going to control all of this land. When the highway comes through, I'm going to be the main developer of this entire area."

"What does that have to do with me?"

"I want you to be a part of it."

"I'm not much of a land developer."

"What do you make a year at that PI job of yours?"

"Enough to get by."

"Wouldn't you like to do better? Wouldn't you like to get in on the ground floor of the next big thing? Wouldn't you like to be rich?"

"Depends on what it costs me."

"Your investment would be minimal at best, a formality."

"I wasn't talking about money."

"Frankie, I'm giving you the chance to get in on something that will change your life forever. This is the chance of a lifetime."

"What's the catch?"

"What catch? There is no catch. Can't I look out for a good friend?"

Bradley was looking at me like I was crazy. Maybe I was. He couldn't understand why I wasn't jumping on his offer. Part of me was wondering the same thing. It's not like I had anything against money, especially easy money.

Everything seemed a little too convenient, a little too much like a bribe.

"What do you want from me?"

"I don't want anything from you."

"Everybody around here wants something."

"Remember who you're talking to here. I'm the guy who served alongside of you in the war. I'm the one who saved your life." It was the first time he'd ever played that card.

"Yeah, that you did and I owe you for that one, but if you think that means I'm going to lay back and let you walk all over people maybe you should have left me floating in the water that day."

"Why are you being so difficult?"

"Why are you trying to buy me off?"

"I'm just trying to help you out."

"Let's talk about Katherine."

"There's nothing to talk about."

"Don't play me for a sap, Bradley. There's too much going on around here for that. There are a lot of necks in a lot of nooses."

"What can I tell you? When I broke it off with Katherine she took it pretty hard. She couldn't accept the fact that I was in love with Lucy."

"That doesn't explain you and her now."

"There's nothing to explain. I've spent some time with her, trying to console her, make her understand that it's over between us, that there's no chance we could ever be together again. Despite what you might think, I still care about her. I want her to be happy."

It wasn't flying in my head, but I doubted I was going to get him to come off his story. There were a lot of pieces to the puzzle that weren't fitting in place.

"What about Gilbert, he's in on this deal, isn't he?"

Bradley hesitated. "This deal I have working is at a very sensitive time right now. I really can't discuss the details. You're just going to have to trust me on this. I need you to back off on all that for awhile."

"That's it, isn't it? That's what you want from me. You want me to let up and stop making waves."

"It's not like that at all. I just want to make sure you're on my side."

"You realize a man's dead, right? A man you worked alongside of. I wouldn't think there should be any sides where that's concerned."

Bradley didn't answer.

"You know, I think you're a lot more like the old man than you admit. Secret deals, cover ups and buy offs, what's next? Stealing farms from working class stiffs? Robbing your friends of land and selling it to the government? Marrying a beautiful woman and turning her into a vegetable?"

Bradley was quick. I hardly had time to react when he'd grabbed me by the lapels and charged into me, hurling me backwards and slamming me into the hood of his car. He had me lying across it, hovering over me, his left hand holding me down, his right clenched in a fist and poised to slug me.

"Go ahead," I said. "I'm not your old man but I'll do in a pinch. It's what you've always wanted to do, isn't it? It's why you're so hell bent on sticking it to the old bastard, some payback for what he did to your mother."

"Don't you say anything about her. She's a sick woman."

"She's sick all right. Sick with heartache and torment, of having the life sucked out of her, sick with years of covering her pain with hardcore narcotics. He's the one that did it to her."

"You don't know what you're talking about."

"Don't I? Isn't it the same thing you're doing to Katherine, controlling her, holding her hostage? Do you think she's the one that will end up like Mommy or do you think it will be Lucy after years of suffering through a loveless marriage, you carrying the torch for another woman?"

He let me have it across the left cheek. It sent my head whipping to the side and practically knocked me unconscious. I turned back to him, my head spinning and my sight blurry.

"Is that all you got? I would think you'd have a lot more pent up in there after all these years or maybe you took out the brunt of it on Tucker Morgan already."

Bradley looked confused and stunned. His clenched fist

relaxed and he let his arm fall limp at his side. "You think I killed Tucker?"

"I think you're on the short list of possibilities."

"Why would I do that?"

"Revenge, business, I don't know."

"I didn't kill anybody."

"That night at the hotel, when we were watching the door," I said. "When you reached up and closed it, did you do it because you wanted to stop people from looking at the body, or did you do it because you knew your fingerprints were already on the door? If I saw you touch it I could explain how they got there."

"Is that what you think?"

"You were staying two doors down from Tucker and you told the sheriff you were one of the first ones on the scene but you weren't. You came on the scene late. Where were you?"

Bradley released his grip on me and backed away. "I didn't kill Tucker Morgan."

I was standing up again and rubbing the side of my face where he slugged me. He had a better punch than either Charlie Jackson or Chet Bowman. I would know, being the local punching bag and all.

"I hear that a lot these days."

"You've got to believe me. You know me, Frankie. You know I'm not capable of that."

"Before I came down here there were a lot of things I thought you weren't capable of. Maybe you should take me back to the hotel."

He was moving like a zombie, like he was in a state of shock. Neither of us said a word as we climbed back into the car and headed off. The silence lingered between us the entire ride back to the Ocean Forest.

Part of me was glad I finally let loose with some of the dark thoughts I had creeping around in the back of my skull. Most of me didn't feel so good about it.

I had just accused my best friend of murder, not to mention a few other delicate indiscretions. Things like that don't tend to sit too easy in your gut, especially when it's the guy you owe your hide to.

We pulled up in front of the hotel and Bradley took the car out of gear, leaving the motor running. He looked over at me and said, "I'm sorry for hitting you."

"Forget it."

"What happened to us, Frankie? We used to be such good friends."

"Life, death, dames, money ... who knows?"

"I didn't kill Tucker Morgan," he said. "I swear on my mother's life I didn't do it."

I looked over at him and tried to imagine him the way he was a few years earlier, when we were best friends in the army. I tried to picture him in those army fatigues, dirty and sweaty, marching along with a rifle in his hand. I couldn't. He was a different person now.

Part of me wanted to believe him. Who am I kidding? Every part of me wanted to believe.

Chapter Twenty-Three

*F*reckle Face took me up to my floor, as usual. This time he was on his best behavior, standing at attention and not saying a word. The doors opened and I started to step out but turned back in. There was a cautious look on his face.

For a full thirty seconds I stood perfectly still, staring him down. I could see the perspiration beading up on his forehead, the anxiousness in his eyes.

Suddenly, I lurched slightly forward and said, "Boo!"

Freckle Face jumped two feet in the air, almost hitting his head on the top of the elevator. I smiled, all friendly like, and walked off. What's life without a little fun every once in a while?

Back in my room, I washed my face and took a long look in the mirror. I was beginning to look like a prizefighter. The latest bruise on my cheek was still red and puffy but I knew it would be purple before long.

My jacket and tie were off and my shirt was open, the sleeves rolled up to the elbows. I walked out onto the balcony and stood leaning on the rail.

The sun was sitting low in the west and casting a shadow across the dunes below, extending to almost where the beach began. Only a few scattered beach goers were out, soaking in the late afternoon sunshine, playing in the waves.

She was feisty today. Her waves were coming in bigger than I had seen since I'd been there, crashing about on the shoreline, violent and haphazard. Ripples rolled in from the distance, one after another, a constant barrage of water emanating from some far off spot I couldn't see. The Atlantic was a typical woman, easy and relaxed one day, dangerous and relentless the next. Like any other high spirited girl, you never knew which to expect.

I looked off to the right and tried to find the spot in the dunes where I had been with Katherine the night before. In the daylight it was impossible to tell, everything looked so much different in the light.

I looked off to the left and counted the balconies to the one outside of Tucker Morgan's room. The balconies were spaced out about six or seven feet apart, not a ridiculous distance. It looked like a person could jump from one balcony to the next without breaking their neck, working their way down to where the fire escape began, an iron ladder built into the surface of the south corner of the building. Maybe not someone with a gimp leg like me but someone athletic and healthy like Bradley could do it easily.

There was a telephone in the room and I walked back in and retrieved it. I sat on the corner of the bed with the earpiece in my left hand and the mouthpiece in my right, ringing up the hotel operator.

"Where would you like to call?" she asked in a business-like voice.

"Atlanta, Georgia."

"Who would you like to speak with in Atlanta?"

"I don't know yet. Let's start off with the local newspaper and take it from there, the society page editor."

"One moment please."

Over the next forty-five minutes I talked to three different newspaper men and four of Atlanta's finest. At first nobody could help me and they kept referring me to someone else. Eventually I started getting some answers and I was able to piece a few things together.

Michael Tate was the eldest son of a prominent Atlanta family. From what I gathered, he had been a bit of a playboy who spent much of his youth traveling around the southern states. Sometime about sixteen years ago he had gone off on one of his adventures and never made it back.

It had been quite the stink among the Atlanta socialites, and there were all sorts of rumors floating around. Some said he had met a girl in the Carolinas and run off with her, turning his back on the family fortunes. Others said he had gotten into debt with some mobsters in Florida, gambling debts he couldn't pay back. There was even one that said he had gone west and joined a monastery, forsaking all worldly goods.

Whatever the story, the one thing was for certain, Michael Tate had left home sixteen years ago and never returned. It got the old wheels churning in my head again.

There was no urgency in me as I began to dress myself, once again putting on my second hand tuxedo. My thoughts were somewhere else as I pulled it all together and spiffed myself up as best I could. It's not like I had a lot to work with.

Dinner was being served early tonight, no band or dancing, no reception after. The plan was for everyone to get to bed at a decent time and be refreshed and ready for the morning ceremony. I still had a little time.

Like I'm prone to do, I decided to head down to the bar. I took a little money from the envelope and placed the rest in the bureau. There wouldn't be a need for large amounts of cash tonight.

On the way down, in the elevator, Freckle Face seemed a bit uneasy and on edge, like he was bracing himself for an attack from me. I guess some people are nervous types.

In the Brookgreen Room, a few wedding guests were hanging out at the tables, killing some time before chow was served. I didn't know any of them very well and nobody seemed to pay me any attention as I took a seat at the bar.

My face was stinging and my leg was sore so I proceeded to self medicate in the way that I do. I was on my second shot when Dorothy Jackson came in.

As she walked in, people around the bar took notice, giving her the eye and whispering amongst themselves. It looked like word had gotten around and she noticed it too. To her credit, she held her head high and walked over to the empty seat beside me.

168

She sat down, clutching a dime store romance novel at her chest.

"Can I talk to you?"

"Sure, you want a drink?"

"No thanks. I need to tell you something."

"I'm all ears."

"I guess you've heard the rumors going around, the ones about me and Tuck."

"I've heard some things."

"The police have questioned Charlie three times now. They think he might have killed Tuck."

"What do you think?"

"Charlie didn't kill anybody. He's not like that."

"Jealousy is a pretty powerful motive."

"Look, I don't care what people say about me, let them talk. What do I care? Most of these uppity types are worse than anybody. You wouldn't believe some of the stuff I hear."

"I bet."

"Anyway, they're going to believe what they want. As far as I'm concerned it's nobody's business either way."

"Ok?"

"I hear you're some kind of detective from up north. I hear you're looking into Tuck's murder."

I shrugged. "I've been asking around."

"I did something, something I probably shouldn't have."

"We've all been there."

"A couple of months ago Bradley came to me. I'm the secretary for the whole office and I do work for all of them when they need, even Tuck before he …

"Anyway, Bradley comes to me and he asks me to do him this favor. He wants me to keep an eye out for anything coming in from the state or from the highway commission. He wants me to go through everything that comes in and anything to do with this proposed highway they're thinking of building he wants me to forward to his office."

"That's a little weird."

"He tells me that we need to keep it under wraps and he's the only one who can know about it. He said it all had something to do with this big deal he was working on."

"That didn't send up a red flag?"

"Of course it did, but he promised me that when it was all said and done there was going to be a big bonus in it for me. He was going to give me a commission like I was one of the big boys or something."

"So, you did it."

"Sure I did. Do you know how much I make at that office? It isn't much, I can tell you that. With all the money they make there, why shouldn't I get my share? I work hard for those people."

"Did anybody find out?"

"No. We kept everything between ourselves. Anything that even mentioned anything to do with the highway I sent right to Bradley. Nobody but him and me knew anything about it."

"I guess that's how business is done down here."

"The thing is Tuck and I was friends, good friends. We used to talk and stuff." She looked around the room, nervous like, checking out who was staring at her. "I know what people are saying but they just don't get it. Tucker could be an SOB when it came to business but he was different with me.

"He used to talk to me. He used to listen to me when I said things. He cared about what I thought and he respected my opinion. I used to be able to tell him stuff I couldn't tell other people."

Everything she was saying reminded me of a lot of things I'd heard in my office in Baltimore. "Conversations like that can lead to people getting pretty chummy."

Dorothy straightened herself in her stool, pulling the romance book tight into her body. She was looking away from me, timid about meeting my eyes.

"Well, I started feeling guilty and all about hiding stuff from Tuck. With the way he was with me, I felt like I was betraying him by not telling him. I felt like it was something he needed to know about. I didn't even care about the money anymore."

"You told him?"

"Last week, a few days before we came up for the wedding."

"Anybody else know?"

She shook her head no. "Not that I know of." Dorothy turned back and looked me in the eye. "I don't know if it's important or not but I just thought you might want to know."

"Thanks."

"You're not going to tell anybody are you? I mean I don't care what people think but if it were to get back to Charlie that I … "

"Don't worry. Your secret's safe with me."

She smiled at me but it wasn't a warm or friendly one, it was nervous and awkward, clutching at her cheap romance book. I started to understand a thing or two about Dorothy Jackson, or at least I thought I did.

I figured she was a dreamer, lost in a world of fantasies but stuck in a cruel world where she was forced to sit back and watch while other people made their dreams come true. While Bradley and his father were wheeling and dealing, getting fatter and richer by the minute, Dorothy sat behind a desk and answered phones, filed papers. At the end of the day, she went home to a jealous husband and cooked dinner, cleaned the house and did the laundry.

Maybe those romance novels were all she had, an escape from a bitter reality. Maybe Tucker Morgan had been an escape for her too. Maybe it was why she had given me her maiden name that night I had met her at the bar. Maybe it was all part of the fantasy. I felt sorry for her.

After she left I ordered a drink and another one after that. This whole thing was gnawing at my brain and what-ifs were bouncing around my head like ping pong balls.

The thing that was really getting to me was the way my best friend kept popping up. Why all the secrets and sneaking around? What exactly had Bradley gotten himself in the middle of?

I didn't want to think it but how could I not? Sure, he was my best friend. He was the guy who saved my life and I owed him everything. That's why it was so hard to think that my buddy could be smack dab in the middle of a shit storm.

Everything seemed to fit, the lying and cheating, the sneaking around with Katherine. The secret land deals, the highway running through, the hatred he had for his old man, it all pointed to one thing. Now I had the realization that Bradley had been hiding something from, not only his father, but Tucker Morgan as well. The fact that Tucker Morgan had found out gave him motive. How much would information like that be worth? What would a guy be willing to do to keep something like that under wraps?

It was eating me alive. It couldn't be true. The Bradley Chilton I knew was honest and hardworking, generous and kind. The Bradley Chilton I knew wasn't capable of cheating people out of land or money, conniving his way through crooked business deals. He certainly wasn't capable of murder. I had to have it all wrong.

"Barkeep, I'll take another whiskey," I said.

The bartender gave me a funny look. "You're hitting it pretty hard there, bud. You sure you don't want to take a little break?"

I looked up at him but it was difficult to make him out clearly. Things were starting to get a little fuzzy and the world was spinning around him. "I'm fine," I answered, "just give me another drink."

"Ok, if you're sure."

Chapter Twenty-Four

*M*aybe the bartender was right. By the time I made it in late for dinner I was feeling pretty good. My legs were mush and I was having trouble keeping my balance, half stumbling into the ballroom. I felt clumsy and off kilter as I planted myself into a chair and stared down at the plate in front of me. Tonight it was Veal Cordon Bleu, veal stuffed with ham and served with a rich cheese sauce, tasty stuff. I wolfed it down in no time flat.

The people at my table were looking at me like I had bugs crawling across my face, but I was beyond the point of caring what anyone thought. I had a first rate drunk going and was busy trying to block out the bad things I was thinking about Bradley.

A waiter came by and plopped a piece of key lime pie in front of me. I had it finished off before most of the others had forks in their hands.

With nothing else to occupy myself, I started looking around the ballroom. Bradley was up front at the head table. There was an empty spot beside him where Lucy was supposed to be. He was leaning off to his right, talking with his father. They looked to be in the midst of a serious conversation. At one point, they stopped talking and both of them turned and looked in my direction. They didn't seem too pleased. I figured they had a good idea of how drunk I was.

When they went back to talking I scanned the room, looking for Katherine. She was nowhere to be found. Too bad, an eye full of Katherine Mathews seemed like just what I needed about then.

I wasn't feeling particularly sociable so I decided to excuse myself and head back to the bar for some more mind numbing. As I got up and tripped my way toward the wooden archway leading out, Katherine and Lucy came strolling in. They were arm in arm and leaning in close to each other, speaking privately.

When they saw me approaching they stopped to stare. What was it with these people? You'd think they'd never seen a guy with a load on before.

Katherine turned away as I walked by. She looked upset and maybe a little embarrassed. She could have been crying, I couldn't tell.

Lucy didn't look away. She gave me a cold hard glare, her eyes harsh and angry, her face devoid of anything remotely friendly. She held that look as I walked past. I wasn't entirely sure what was going on, but it was fairly obvious that I had pissed some people off. I guess I should have passed on that last shot of whiskey.

I was working my way through the lobby and toward the stairs leading back down to the Brookgreen Lounge when I felt a hand on my shoulder. I turned around and found Alfred Chilton standing before me. His face was red and clenched. He wasn't happy.

"What exactly do you think you're doing?"

"I thought I was heading to the bar for a night cap," I slurred back.

"I just had a little talk with my son."

"He is getting married tomorrow, it's probably a good time for that 'birds and bees' chat fathers have to give sons."

Chilton ignored my wise crack. "He told me all about the talk you two had earlier."

I was a little surprised. "There were some things that needed to be said."

"Just whose side are you on, anyway?"

"I didn't know we were picking teams."

"This is not at all what I expected when I retained your

services."

"What did you expect?"

"I expected you to do what I asked, not harass my family and employees."

"Yeah, well, no extra charge for that."

"McKeller, this is not acceptable behavior."

"Well, maybe I don't think your behavior is so acceptable either."

"What is that supposed to mean?"

"What do you think it means? No wonder Bradley has himself neck deep in this mess. It's how you raised him, isn't it?"

"Now see here—"

"What's wrong, Alfred? Are you upset that junior is a little too much a chip off the old block?"

"Are you drunk?"

"Crooked land deals, robbing from friends, stealing the homes of hard working families … "

The look on Chilton's face was priceless. For a moment I thought he might have swallowed his tongue. There was no way I could let up now.

"Bradley is just doing what he was taught. Swindling from friends and family, doing whatever it takes to add another jewel to the old crown. You've got to admit he gets it honest. You're the king of swindles and cover ups, aren't you?"

"Have you lost your mind?"

"Alfred, why don't you tell me about how your wife ended up in a narcotic haze? Why don't you tell me what happened to Michael Tate?"

"Michael Tate has nothing to do with anything."

"Michael Tate has everything to do with everything. That's how you people work down here. If somebody gets in your way you plow them over. You don't let anybody get between you and whatever it is you want.

"It's just business, right? Another dollar in the wallet, another plot of land to add to the empire? Anything it takes, just so long as you can keep up appearances while you do it. Just so long as everybody thinks you're the model of respectability. That's what it's all about, isn't it?"

"McKeller, you're talking nonsense."

"Am I? That's why you hired me, isn't it? To keep you and yours out of the skillet? To make sure that nobody in your circle got caught in the middle of an ugly scandal? You never wanted me to find out the truth, you were pretty clear about that from the beginning. You probably suspected that one of yours was mixed up in this somehow. You wanted me to find out for you, to give you the heads up so you could have time to make it go away before it blew up in your face."

"What are you saying?"

"Tucker Morgan was a small price to pay to keep your family name free of dirt. So what if he was a loyal employee for years and years? It's not like he was family or anything. As far as employees go, you can always go out and buy yourself another one."

"Are you saying you believe Bradley is involved in Tucker Morgan's murder?"

"Are you saying he's not?"

"McKeller, you are insane."

"Who had the most to gain? Who was the one running around here, lying, cheating, plotting ... "

"No, no, no—" Chilton had his hands over his ears and was shaking his head back and forth. "I will not stand here and listen to this hog wash. You need to go to your room and sleep it off. We will discuss this matter in the morning when you're sober. Maybe by then you will realize how ridiculous this is."

Chilton stormed off. I was standing there watching him go, wondering how the old bird was going to get through the night with this hanging over his head. I spotted Lucy across the way. She was standing over to the side of the lobby, near the ballroom entrance, like she had been waiting for Chilton to finish with me before approaching. She came over.

I could tell by the look on her face that she was angry but I underestimated just how angry she was. The slap across my face came as a surprise.

"What was that for?" I asked, rubbing my cheek with my hand.

"We trusted you, Frankie. We invited you down here to be a part of our special day. We treated you like you were a part of our family."

"I'm guessing I screwed it up somehow."

"Katherine is a part of our family as well."

Now I was really confused. "This has something to do with Katherine?"

"You know of her history with Bradley. You know that she probably harbors feelings for him in some way, how could she not?"

"I'm not following you."

"She asked me not to say anything but I couldn't help myself. I need you to know how disappointed I am with the way you have behaved."

"This is not at all the way I thought this conversation would go."

"Katherine is a sweet and innocent girl and she was feeling a bit vulnerable, maybe a little depressed, it's not surprising."

"So, this is about Katherine and me?"

"You took advantage of her situation, Frankie. You ought not to have done that. We have a name for men who do such things down here."

"What would that be?"

Lucy took a deep breath. I could only imagine the name she was thinking of. Obviously, it was beneath her to utter it aloud.

"You have betrayed our trust and in the process you have hurt a dear member of our family. What you have done is beyond contempt."

"Yeah, I got that part."

"I would prefer if you didn't attend our ceremony tomorrow," she said callous and cold like it was the stiffest punishment imaginable.

"You're uninviting me to the wedding?"

"I haven't discussed it with Bradley. I know that the two of you are very close and he doesn't know about what happened yet. I would rather not tell him. I think it would be better if you were to return to Baltimore."

"Just slink out in the middle of the night with my tail between my legs?"

"I'll tell him that something came up, an emergency back

home."

"I don't understand why what happened between Katherine and me has anything to do with you. To be honest, I'm more than a little surprised that she chose to tell you about it."

"Katherine and I have been the dearest of friends for years."

"It's funny, I never really got that. Things always seemed a little tense between the two of you from what I saw."

"Don't be silly. We are the best of friends."

"Does she often come to you with such personal dilemmas?"

"She was upset, as you can imagine. She needed someone to talk to."

"And she chose to come to you, the fiancé of her old boyfriend?"

You could slice tomatoes with the look she was giving me. "I think it would be best for everyone involved if you weren't here in the morning."

"Yeah, well, the thing is I really love weddings. They always make me cry."

"You are not welcome at the ceremony."

There it was, all blunt and brutal. I had gone from friend of the family to outsider, just like that. She didn't even know that I suspected her husband to be was involved in Tucker Morgan's death. Imagine what she would have thought of me then.

Lucy turned and walked away. She held her head up straight and her shoulders back, the picture of refinement and sophistication. She was oozing decorum.

I no longer felt like a drink. Well, maybe I did but my better judgment told me it wasn't a good idea. It's not very often I hear from better judgment. He and I have a shaky relationship at best.

I decided to turn in.

Chapter Twenty-Five

Up in my room, I sat on the corner of the bed with my jacket off. I was trying to put all the pieces together in my mind, trying to figure out where everything went so wrong. I felt like garbage.

In a few short days I had taken the best friendship I'd ever had and turned it into a pile of dung. He was the guy responsible for me seeing the light of day the past two years and I had turned on him. I'd made enemies of his friends and family.

What in hell was I thinking? I had no business sticking my nose where it didn't belong. I wasn't even a real detective and there I was poking around in a murder case, accusing my buddy of the unthinkable.

It's not like I really had anything to go on, a lot of hearsay and circumstantial evidence. I couldn't even figure out how it all went together. Maybe it didn't. Maybe I was in too far over my head to see that I didn't have a clue. Like I said, I suck at this job.

I kept going back to Katherine, that night on the beach, the day at the racetrack. The things she had said to me, the way she treated me after, the fact that she had told Lucy about us. None of it made any sense. I guess the one thing I knew less about than detective work was women.

Lying back on the bed and staring up and the ceiling, the

patterned wallpaper, I kept replaying it all in my head, watching it like it was a movie. Trying to figure it all out and see where I had screwed everything up.

I'm a pretty dense guy when it comes to most things. I'm not exactly sure when or how the thought came to me. It crept into my head like some timid hobo getting up the courage to beg for change. It got in there and made me look at it from every angle, daring me to shoot it down. I couldn't. That's how I figured out what was up with Katherine Mathews.

Without even bothering to put my jacket on, I rushed out of my room and to the elevator. Freckle Face was waiting for me when the doors opened. He looked scared but I barely noticed.

"Fourth floor," I said.

Part of me was wondering if this was a good idea or not, if maybe the booze was affecting my judgment. I stood outside of Katherine's door for a good five minutes, going over in my head what I was going to say. Finally, I knocked.

It took her a little time to answer the door. When she did, she was in a pale green night gown, a thin white robe over it. Her hair was messy and out of place, hanging in her face. Her eyes were tired and red but still had that familiar sparkle to them and her face looked thin and flushed.

"I know," I said as she opened the door.

"You know what?"

"I know what you were talking about. I know what you were apologizing for."

"It's late, Frankie."

"You're pregnant."

Her eyes got wide and her cheeks turned pink, her mouth falling open with a gasp. She didn't answer.

"That's why you were with me that night. That's why you felt so bad for what you did to me. You kept saying you were sorry, but I didn't know what you were talking about. You told Lucy about us, so nine months from now, when the baby comes, she'll think it's mine."

Katherine still didn't answer.

"You knew that Lucy suspected something between you and Bradley. When you found out you were pregnant you had to come up with a story. It would ruin everything if she knew that you had been seeing Bradley this whole time."

"I don't know what you're talking about," she said but her voice sounded distant and unconvincing.

"I was just an alibi. A cover for yours and Bradley's little indiscretion. What I don't get is why go to all this trouble? If you two want to be together, just do it."

She started to say something in protest but it came out all stuttered and incoherent.

"Are you going to deny it?" The sleepy was gone from her eyes and she stood there staring at me with the kind of look on her face you get when somebody beans you in the back of the head with a two by four. "That day at the pool, you weren't sick from drinking. You barely touched your mint julep the night before. It was morning sickness."

"Frankie, no, you're wrong."

"Am I? Look me in the eye and tell me you didn't sleep with me to cover up the fact you're carrying Bradley's child."

"That's the craziest thing I've ever heard."

"I know but it doesn't make it any less true."

Katherine reached over and rested her right hand on my shoulder, guiding it down and around the top of my arm. Her touch made the rest of me tingle.

"You're upset," she said with a sigh, her voice all gentle and soothing. "You're talking crazy."

She stepped into me, turning her head to the side, and leaned in, placing her face against my chest. The building started spinning and I could feel the heat coming off her, mixing with mine. It reminded me of the night on the beach.

Her hands were on my back, making small tender circles on my skin with her fingers. Instinctively, I wrapped my arms around her and pulled her body into mine, holding her tight against me. My breathing was deep and labored and my head felt like it was filled with oatmeal.

Katherine lifted her head and looked up at me, those deep brown eyes seeping into my eye sockets and flooding my brain. Every sense I had seemed to be connected directly to her in some way. I could feel every inch of her flesh where it was pressed up somewhere against me or brushed past when she moved. The smell of her was overwhelming, a mild mix of diluted perfume, salt air and bed sheets. Even my ears were filled with her, the soft rhythm of her breathing, the gentle sighs she let out, the rustling of her nightgown. There was only one thing missing.

I reached down and took her perfect face in my hands, pulling her into me and kissing her hard on the mouth. She tasted like warm mint cookies and I could feel myself melt away in her arms.

There was no longer anything resembling self control inside of me. I was lost in her, kissing frantically about her face and mouth, groping and pawing at her body, a hopeless junkie in need of another fix of Katherine Mathews.

She pulled her face back a few inches and gazed up at me. "You can come in if you'd like," she said in a low whisper.

We were still locked in tight embrace as we shuffled our way through the doorway, me kissing her neck, her running her fingers along the back of my head. I slammed the door behind us and continued to guide her across the room, to the foot of the bed.

Katherine pushed herself away from me and let herself fall back across the bed and I stood over her, gawking at the sight. She raised her torso up on her elbows and peeled the robe off her shoulders, letting it fall in a puddle beneath her. The nightgown she was wearing was thin and almost transparent, clinging to every curve of her, accentuating her form.

She raised her left leg and rubbed her calf up the length of mine. As she did, the nightgown fell away, exposing her leg to the thigh and I studied it as she worked it up and down, inviting me to take her. It was long and lean, slightly thick at the thigh and working down to thin, toned calf muscles and skinny ankles, perfect feet with high arches, pointed out at the toes.

I'm not exactly sure when or why reality and common sense decided to show back up. I'm not even sure I wanted them to. Part of me wanted to tell them to take a hike and come back later, but a little voice started going off in my head. I hate that little voice.

There I was with the woman of my dreams throwing herself

at me, practically begging me to have my way with her. It was a done deal. All I had to do was pull the trigger. Something wouldn't let me.

Sure, I wanted her. I wanted her more than anything I had ever wanted before but not like this. It was Chilton handing me an envelope stuffed with money. It was Bradley inviting me in on his big land deal. I was being bought off.

While it was maybe the nicest possible way to be bought off, it was being bought off just the same. Katherine was willing to whore herself out to me in exchange for me keeping my mouth shut, forgetting what I knew. I picked a hell of a time to discover morals and decency.

"No," I said.

Katherine stopped with the leg rubbing and gave me a funny look. She wasn't the kind of dame who was used to hearing no from any man, especially in this situation.

"What?"

"No," I said again. "I can't do this."

She got suddenly embarrassed and sat up on the bed, gathering her nightgown around her and slipping back into the robe. "You didn't have any problem the other night," she said and her voice had a sharp angry tone to it.

"Yeah, well, we both know that was under false pretenses."

Katherine stood up and pulled the robe in around her neck, covering as much of her body as she could. "Why are you doing this?"

"I guess I just don't like being played."

"Is that what you think this is? Is that the kind of person you think I am?"

"Do you really want me to answer that?"

She was dumbstruck, and she stood looking at me with a shocked and exasperated expression. I backed my way to the door, still soaking in every second of her, still regretting my decision.

"You know, if you were half as beautiful on the inside as you are on the outside, you'd really have something."

Katherine didn't answer but stood glaring at me, covered in disbelief. There was a sad, lost look in her eye like I had let her down or hurt her in some mean way. Maybe it was just the reflection from mine. Maybe it was all in my head.

"Tell your boyfriend we need to talk tomorrow, early, before he takes his vows."

With that I let myself out and went back to my room. I still had no idea what I was doing.

Chapter Twenty-Six

*T*he walk back to my room was long. I took the stairs, forgoing another ride in the elevator with Freckle Face. I was in a daze the whole way, still in shock at my own stupidity. I had made some lunkhead moves before but turning down Katherine Mathews in the heat of passion was the lunkiest. The odds of me ever ending up with a dame on that scale again were on par with me hitting a homerun in the bottom of the ninth to win the World Series. It just isn't going to happen.

At my door, I fumbled for my key and inserted it into the slot. I had just gotten it unlocked and was opening the door when someone slammed into me from behind. The door went flying open and I fell face down on the floor. He was on my back with a knee in my spine and sucker punching me in the kidneys.

There was a jolt to the back of my head and my face rammed into the carpet. It felt like my jaw might have cracked and I could feel the rug burns across my cheek. Whatever he'd hit me with had been heavy and harder than a man's fist and it knocked me silly.

Things were blurry and confused and I was fighting to stay conscious as I felt someone lift me by the shirt collar and stand me up. I wasn't standing long before he ran me face first into the wooden bureau across the room.

I tried to take a swing at him but I was disoriented and groggy, missing completely. He turned me around and leaned me back on the dresser. Chet Bowman had a big smile under his bandaged nose.

"Remember me?"

The knee to my groin sent me doubled over and clutching at my gut. The elbow to the back of the head put me down. Paybacks are a bitch.

It's hard to say how many times he kicked me while I was laying there. He put a foot to my face a few times before going down and kicking me in the stomach a few more. He seemed pretty content to repeat this process over and over.

I was gasping for air and trying to cover up as best I could but my reflexes left a lot to be desired. I still hadn't recovered from that first blow to the head and I was trying to figure out what was happening. Every once in a while I would take a stab at his leg but he was too quick for me.

As far as ambushes and ass kickings go, this one was first rate. I never had a chance.

When he'd had enough, he rolled me over on my back and squatted down beside me. "You really should get that nose looked at."

"Is there something in particular you wanted or did you just stop by to catch up on old times?" I managed to grunt out. For shits and giggles he slugged me in the mouth.

"I'll do the talking here."

I spit some blood onto the carpet and coughed.

"Here's the deal, McKeller, your wedding invitation has expired."

"Darn, I so love a nice wedding."

Bowman cold cocked me on the side of the head.

"You're leaving, tonight. I want you gone by morning."

"Does Chilton pay you extra for this or is this one of your regular duties?"

"Nobody wants you here. If you know what's good for you, you'll disappear."

"Chet, I'm beginning to think you don't like me."

Bowman hit me a couple more times, once in the face and

another in the gut. I was at the point where I hardly felt it anymore.

"Don't screw with me, McKeller."

I was wincing pretty good, holding my gut and trying to catch my breath. "No, I wouldn't want to screw with you, Chet. I know how sensitive you are about that kind of stuff."

This time he smiled as he bitch slapped me across the face. "You're a funny guy, McKeller, always with the wise cracks, a regular comedian."

"I aim to please."

Bowman was squatted over me, his arms on his knees. "You don't want to be here in the morning. It wouldn't be a good thing."

"Then what would I do with the new toaster I got Bradley and Lucy for a wedding present?"

"I got a pretty good idea where you can stick it."

"Chet, you made a funny. I think you're making real progress."

Bowman grabbed me by the face and squeezed my cheeks in his meaty paws. "This isn't open for discussion. There's a ten o'clock train leaving for Conway, you can get another train heading north from there. You don't want to miss that train."

I was all out of wise cracks and laid there looking up at Chet Bowman. My left eye was beginning to swell shut and my face was throbbing. Aches and pains were shooting through my chest and gut. All I could do was give a quick nod.

"That's better," he said, grinning down at me.

The gig was up. I didn't have any more fight left in me.

Chet let go of my face and I flopped onto the floor, lying limp and motionless.

"There won't be any reason to contact anyone before you go. I'll be sure to pass on your goodbyes."

With my eyes closed, I lay, concentrating on my breathing and listening to Chet Bowman let himself out. I didn't have the strength to get off the floor and climb into bed. Every part of me was throbbing with pain.

Even through the pain I kept thinking of my friend Bradley. I had come a long way in three days. On the train down I had a best friend, a guy I trusted, and the man who saved my life. Now I was going home alone, with the suspicion that the guy I once loved was a murderer.

Maybe leaving was the best thing for everyone. I still owed Bradley my life and I wasn't sure I wanted any part of seeing him sent up the river. As far as I knew, I was the only person who suspected Bradley. If I was out of the picture it would be safer for him.

I was having a hard time stomaching the idea of Bradley getting away with murder but, like I said, I owed him my life. What's a guy supposed to do? Maybe me disappearing was the way to play it. I wasn't really helping him but, at the same time, I wasn't going to be the one to call him out. I wasn't going to be the guy who turned him over.

For a long time I laid there thinking, pondering everything that had happened, everything I knew. Eventually I passed out.

Chapter Twenty-Seven

The sun was up by the time I came to. Judging by the way I felt, I hadn't been out for very long. I woke in the same spot on the floor with my head in a puddle of dried blood and drool.

Pulling myself up to my feet, I limped over to the bathroom and took a long look at myself in the mirror. It wasn't a pretty sight.

My left eye was completely closed, the entire side of my face swollen and purple. The right side wasn't much better, sporting a shiner that any boxer would be proud of.

I cleaned up as best I could and changed clothes, picked up my fedora and sat it low on my head, hoping to hide my bruised face as much as possible. The smart thing to do was to grab a cab and make for that morning train Chet Bowman had told me about, but I wasn't feeling much like smart decisions. Maybe it was having my brains rattled around my head the night before.

In the elevator, Freckle Face was on duty again. When the doors opened he looked like he'd seen a ghost, and he spent the entire ride down trying not to make eye contact with me. I didn't have the energy to screw with him.

As we reached the main level and the doors opened I started out but Freckle Face stopped me.

"Are you OK, mister?"

I stopped and looked back at the kid. There was a look on his face that bordered on genuine concern. Maybe I had him pegged wrong all along.

"I'm fine," I said, smiling through swollen lips. "I cut myself shaving is all."

From there I made my way through the lobby, ignoring the funny looks I was getting along the way. You would think the patrons of the Ocean Forest had never seen a guy with ground beef for a face before.

Out back, on the patio, was the usual assortment of guests enjoying their hearty breakfast and laughing amongst themselves. Off to the side, at a table by himself, was Bradley. He looked a little nervous and fidgety and he was nursing a glass of tomato juice. On second thought, maybe it was a Bloody Mary. I walked up and took a seat.

His eyes nearly bugged out of his head when he caught a gander of me.

"What on earth happened to you?"

"As if you don't know."

"I don't know what you're talking about."

"Let's stop playing games, Bradley. You win. I'm out of here. I'll be on the first train I can catch heading north. You won't have to worry about me messing up your perfect little wedding ceremony, or your perfect little life, for that matter."

"Who did this to you?"

I lit a cigarette and leaned back in my chair, peering up at him from under the brim of my hat. He didn't look like my best friend anymore.

"You did this to me."

He started to say something but I cut him off, my words full of force and fire. "You did this to me when you brought me down here. When you stuck me in the middle of this pretentious bunch of egg heads you call friends and family.

"What did you expect, Bradley? Did you think I was going to sit back and buy into all this bullshit? Did you think that because you treated me like I was a friend I would stand by and let you do whatever you wanted?"

"What are you talking about?"

"You people, with all your money and privilege, you think you're entitled to do whatever you want. You think you can use and manipulate people to whatever means you have in mind. You think that if you take a sap like me and throw him in the middle of your grand lifestyle, with your country clubs and galas and afternoon dips in the ocean, you think that means you own me.

"Everything was fine when I was your flunky buddy from the army but when I started questioning your methods, when I started poking my nose where it wasn't wanted, things changed. The last thing you needed was some blue collared lunk like me upsetting the delicate plan you had laid out for yourself."

"You're talking crazy."

"Yeah, well, maybe I am and maybe I'm not. Either way, you won't have to worry about me anymore. You win, Bradley. I'm not going to be the one who exposes you for what you really are. Maybe I owe you that much but, from here on out, all bets are even. The score is settled. I don't owe you anything anymore."

"You never did owe me anything."

He was throwing out the modesty card again. This time it just pissed me off.

"I don't know what bites my ass worse, the fact that you thought you could bring me down here and dazzle me with your status quo, or the fact you thought you could buy me off so easy. Maybe it was the fact that you and your girlfriend thought I was such a gullible dweeb that you could use me however you wanted. I guess you never figured on me peeking behind the curtain."

"It's not like that at all."

"Maybe you never cared if I peeked or not. After all, you saw me on that day. You saw first hand the kind of person I really am. Maybe that's why you never figured on me getting in the way. You knew all along I didn't have the stomach to rock the boat. Once a coward always a coward, right, Bradley?"

"Is that what you think?"

"That's the way it is. You were right about me. I'm getting out and I'm not going to be the one gumming up the works for you."

"Do you even remember that day?"

I didn't answer. There was no need.

Bradley leaned in over the table, pulling himself in as close as it would allow. He looked around, quick and nervous, making sure no one was within ear shot. When he spoke, his voice was low and serious.

"You had been sick for a week, delirious with fever. You could barely walk. I begged you to go on sick call but you wouldn't hear of it. You weren't going to miss the invasion for anything.

"The two of us made a pact the night before. We were going to get through it together, whatever it took. The plan was for you to stick by my side the entire time. My job was to get you to the beach.

"In the landing craft, I had you by the arm. When they dropped the ramp things were crazy, bullets flying, and explosions everywhere. I was the one who panicked. I ran. I let go of you and I ran diving off into the water. I even lost my rifle.

"When I came up and looked back you were pinned up against the side of the craft, wedged in with all the other guys fighting to get out. I had just started back for you when the shell hit. I thought you were dead."

Bradley sat back in his chair and neither of us said anything for a long while.

"You still saved my life."

"I had to. I couldn't live with the guilt if you had died."

"It doesn't change anything."

"It changes everything, Frankie. You weren't the coward that day. Hell, you shouldn't have even been there. All I had to do was not let go of your arm."

I didn't know what to say. It wasn't like my brain wasn't already filled with scrambled eggs.

"We were friends, Frankie," he half smiled at me.

"Good friends," I added.

"What happened?"

"It was easier back then."

I stood up and walked away, not quite sure how I still felt about Bradley Chilton. What did it really matter? I was about to close that chapter of my life.

Chapter Twenty-Eight

*T*he plan was to go back up to my room, gather my belongings and get the hell out of South Carolina. Plans don't always work out the way they're drawn up.

I hadn't even made it back inside the hotel when I was cut off by Sheriff Talbert. He was with two of his deputies and old man Chilton. Chet Bowman was bringing up the rear. By the look in his eyes, I should have known the good sheriff had something on his mind but his words caught me off guard just the same.

"Frank McKeller, you're under arrest for the murder of Tucker Morgan."

My first instinct was to laugh.

"I'm glad you find this so funny. Cuff him, boys," he said.

One deputy grabbed an arm, twisting it around behind me while the other slapped on a pair of handcuffs. It seemed to me like they were enjoying their chore a little too much, and I ended up with my hands behind me, the cuffs digging into the bones of my wrists.

"This is crazy."

A crowd was gathering around me, all the familiar faces of the weekend. They were filing out of the hotel and forming a circle around the chained freak in the middle.

"Why would I kill Tucker Morgan?"

Sheriff Talbert pulled a white envelope from his pocket with the Chilton letterhead stenciled in the left hand corner. I recognized it at once.

"Money for starters," the sheriff said with a grin. "You got any idea what's in here?"

"A bunch of cash?"

"Just shy of fifteen hundred. That's just short of what Tucker Morgan was supposed to be carrying on him."

"What a coincidence."

"Want to guess where we found it?"

"I'm going to go out on a limb and say my hotel room."

"You're a pretty smart fellow."

I looked over to the old man. "I don't suppose you want to explain to the sheriff where I got that, do you?"

"I have no idea what he's talking about," Chilton replied.

"I figured as much."

People were still filtering out onto the patio deck. I spotted just about everyone from the wedding, minus maybe the bride and her mother.

"I don't suppose you'd believe me if I told you there wasn't more than eight hundred in there last night," I tried.

"Probably not."

"And if I told you that Mr. Chilton paid me that money to look into what was going on here?"

"I would find that rather hard to believe."

"Where did you get the tip to go searching my room, Mr. Chilton?"

"Let's just say we have our sources."

"Look, Sheriff, I'm being framed. It's obvious."

"There's a new one, an accused man claiming his innocence."

"I didn't kill anybody."

"Take him away, boys."

The deputies each had me by an arm and they began to push me through the crowd, making the extra effort to twist my wrists against the handcuffs and sending a surge of pain up my arms. I planted my feet and fought back as best I could.

Lucy and her mother came running out the door about then and everyone stopped, mortified by the sight of the bride out in public just hours before the nuptials. Seeing her hours before the ceremony in full wedding regalia seemed odd at best and I couldn't help picturing her up in her room, ready to go, counting down the minutes before becoming Mrs. Bradley Chilton. I guess she came running downstairs when she heard about the ruckus involving me.

Just the same, I have to admit, Lucy looked stunning, like she'd stepped off a wedding cake. The gown was long and white, silky and shimmering, lacy and luxurious. Her hair was up and tucked in under her veil with a few strands spraying out and hanging at the side of her face.

"Isn't it bad luck for the groom to see the bride before the wedding?" I asked her.

"I believe its bad luck to have your wedding guests murdered too," she answered without missing a beat, a bit of a snarl in her voice.

People were looking at me like my slip was showing and I was beginning to realize the severity of my situation. I was being set up to take the big fall and the set up had some serious financial backing behind it. I got the sense that once they took me away I was never coming back. I had to act fast. I had to come up with something or else I was going to be left holding the bag.

The deputies started to force me through the crowd but I held fast as best I could, fighting them for all I was worth. "I didn't kill Tucker Morgan."

"Tell it to the judge," a deputy said to me.

"Wait! I know who did kill Tucker Morgan."

Sheriff Talbert held up a hand and everybody stopped. I had their attention.

"I can tell you right here and now who murdered Tucker Morgan."

"I'm listening."

I shook loose of the deputies hold and stood as straight as I could, trying to work my wrists in a position where the pain was bearable. Looking around the crowd, I tried to figure out what to do next. This wasn't the plan. I had to buy some time.

Gilbert Fleming was giving me the evil eye. It was as good a place to start as any. I stepped in front of him, staring him

195

back down.

"I think it's fair to say that you were the first suspect."

He didn't respond.

"You were arguing with Tucker the night he was killed. Would you care to tell us what the argument was about?"

Still no answer.

"You certainly had motive to kill Tucker Morgan. Tucker was at least partially responsible for your family's recent misfortunes. It was Tucker who found the land deal that led to the army air field. He was the one who suggested Chilton buy the land from your father and it was Tucker who turned around and sold it to the government."

"You're crazy."

"That little deal cost your family quite a bit of change. It might have been enough to get your family back in good standing."

"Our family is in quite good standing," Herbert Fleming cut in. I glanced over at the old bird. He looked stiff and uncomfortable, small signs of embarrassment across his features.

"That would give you motive too, Mr. Fleming."

Herbert Fleming stiffened some more and his eyes bugged out a bit.

"Murder isn't really your style, is it?"

No answer.

"Besides, you aren't the one that was in two heated arguments with the victim the night he was killed. That would be Gilbert." I glared back at the son. "The thing is, the air field wasn't your only beef with Tucker Morgan. In fact, you were more concerned with the deal you were working on than anything that happened in the past. You wanted to see that Tucker didn't interfere with the one you had in the works."

"If you have an accusation to make, make it."

"Aside from the argument, there were the lies, plenty of them too. You lied about what the two of you were arguing about. You lied about where you were. You even lied about walking back to your room with Lucy."

I turned back to the crowd. "The thing is Gilbert has an alibi for the night. He was in the company of a certain young lady at one of Myrtle Beach's more seedy drinking establishments. The reason for the big cover up? Gilbert's lady friend happens to suffer from a very serious condition. It's called marriage to another fellow."

The crowd started murmuring, another skeleton out of the closet.

"It would appear that Gilbert Fleming is in the clear. That is, unless he and his girl are lying."

Off to the right and standing close together were Charlie and Dorothy Jackson. They averted their gaze when I looked at them. I walked over and stood in front of the couple.

"The next suspect was Charlie Jackson. We've all heard the rumors, the murmurings that there might have been more between Tucker and Dorothy than just business. Jealousy is a strong motive for murder."

The two were squirming and shifting uncomfortably, Dorothy's face turning a deep shade of pink. Charlie lifted his chin and slid his arm around his wife, pulling her in tight against him, standing tall and defiant against my accusations.

"The thing is, I looked extensively into this particular scenario, it being the most obvious and all. Jealousy is a strong motive for murder but I investigated this option thoroughly and what I found was it was all a bunch of hooey.

"There was no affair between Tucker Morgan and Dorothy Jackson. They were two coworkers and probably very good friends. Everything else is all talk. There's nothing to it."

I couldn't help but glance back over at the couple. They seemed to be standing a little taller than before, arm in arm, a united front. Of course my entire proclamation about the non-affair between Tucker and Dorothy was a load of horse shit. If anything, I suspected the opposite was true. I'm not even sure why I said it. Maybe I had been on the other end, tearing marriages apart, for so long I wanted to see what it was like to help put one back together for a change. Either way, I was pretty sure that neither of them had anything to do with Tucker Morgan's murder.

"This is enough of this nonsense. I demand you take this criminal into custody." It was old man Chilton throwing his two cents in. He was at the front of the circle, standing next to the missus.

197

I strolled over and stood in front of him, staring into his angry old eyes. There was a look on his face like he wanted to punch me in the gut, which he could have easily done what with my hands cuffed behind my back.

"I would have really liked it if had been you, Mr. Chilton. Nothing would give me more pleasure than to stand here and announce that you killed Tucker Morgan."

"I'm sure that you would but the mere idea that I might have something to do with Tucker's killing is preposterous," he huffed back at me.

"Yeah, that's not really your style, is it? You're more suited to barking orders and pulling strings. No wonder half this town has it out for you."

"I'll have you know I'm one of the most respected men in these parts."

"Respected or feared? Everyone knows how powerful you are, how much money you have but that's not really the same as being respected. You're good at acquiring property and turning profits, at stealing the land of hard working Americans and turning them out on the streets but that isn't respect."

"You don't know what you're talking about."

"How about your son's future father in-law, does he respect you after you bought his land for pennies on the dollar and turned around and sold it to the Feds for big bucks? Is that how you treat your friends?"

"Sheriff, I demand you do something about this man."

I ignored Chilton's plea to the sheriff and continued on. "What about your son, Chilton? Does he respect you? Is that why he's plotting behind your back to break from your company and branch out on his own? Is it out of respect that he would do anything to get out from under your grip?"

"That's ridiculous."

"And what about your wife, Chilton, how much does she respect you? Is that why she drowns herself in a sea of narcotics, because of the respect she has for you?"

The old man's face was blood red and the veins in his temples looked like they might burst at any moment. You could almost see the steam coming out of his ears.

"Tell me about Michael Tate."

"There's nothing to tell."

"What happened to Michael Tate?"

Those old eyes locked on mine and he shot me the kind of glare reserved the lowest of the low, like I was so far beneath him I wasn't worth the effort it would take to spit on. "You had better watch your step, McKeller. You're on very dangerous ground."

How much more dangerous could it get? I already had a murder rap hanging over my head. I turned to Sheriff Talbert. "It's a little late to open an investigation but there was a guy by the name of Tate. He disappeared fifteen or twenty years ago. You could probably check with the Atlanta authorities.

"Michael Tate was a friend of Mrs. Chilton. Apparently, Mr. Chilton thought they were a little too friendly. He and Chet Bowman took care of that little problem."

Mrs. Chilton let out a noise that sounded somewhere between a shriek and a squeal and her body went limp, people around her catching her before she hit the ground. Who knew she could even understand English under the heavy dosage of medication she was always under?

They ushered her over to a chair and brought her a glass of water while some of the other ladies fanned her face and loosened her collar. Mr. Chilton was up in the sheriff's face. "I demand you remove this man from the premises before he does any further damage. His lies are hurtful and libelous and it is outright negligence for you to allow this to continue."

There was a lot of commotion and talking, voices lapping over other voices, a sense of hysteria running through the crowd. I got the sense that the sheriff was ready to give in and haul me away when everyone began to stop and look back over to Harriet Chilton. She was sitting up in the chair and mumbling softly.

"Poor ... dear ... sweet Michael. He was such a lovely man."

"That's enough, Harriet," Chilton ordered.

She looked up at her husband but it didn't look like she even recognized him. "I tried to tell Alfred there was nothing improper about our relationship but he wouldn't listen. Michael was such a dear sweet friend. We would just sit out on the terrace and drink

199

tea and talk for hours and hours. I so loved spending time with him. He was the dearest friend."

"What happened to Michael?" I asked.

Harriet Chilton's face went from soft and loving to stone. She looked at me like I had just uttered the foulest of curse words. "Alfred wouldn't allow us to be friends."

"That is quite enough," Chilton snapped.

"Let the lady speak," the sheriff replied to the old man.

"What happened to Michael?" I asked again.

"My wife is a very sick woman."

The sheriff took Alfred Chilton by the arm and turned him to face him. The forced politeness was gone from his voice and there was a slight grin on his face like he was enjoying the scene. "Mr. Chilton, if you don't pipe down I'll run you in for obstruction of justice."

"Harriet, what happened to Michael Tate?" I asked for a third time.

Mrs. Chilton let her body relax, her shoulders falling forward and slumping in her chair. Her eyes were glassed over and her face had the look of someone far away. She let out a long sigh that bordered on a moan, as though she were about to release something evil and painful from her body.

"There was a fight. Alfred was so angry. He was certain that there was something between Michael and me. We tried to ease his fears. We assured him that we were just friends. Alfred hit me. Michael came to my defense.

"There was a scuffle. Michael had Alfred against the fireplace, had him pinned to the wall. Alfred reached up and grabbed the silver candlestick from the mantle—"

"My wife is heavily sedated. She doesn't know what she's saying."

"That's enough out of you, Chilton," the sheriff warned again.

"Harriet," I tried in my softest voice. "Where is Michael now?"

She cocked her head to the side and looked at me as if I'd just asked the silliest question ever. "Why, Michael is where he always is. He's out behind the greenhouse. I visit him every day."

The crowd let out a collective gasp.

I sneaked a quick peek over to Bradley. He was looking on at the scene like what he was witnessing wasn't quite registering in his brain. Hate the old man or not, I guess he never figured him for a murderer.

"My wife suffers from a very severe illness. The medication sometimes makes her say things … " Chilton was trying to explain but he wasn't very convincing. His face had gone from blood red to ghostly white and it looked like the confidence he was never without had been bled out of him.

Sheriff Talbert turned to one of his deputies. "Call the Charleston authorities and have them send some men out to the Chilton estate. Tell them to check the area behind the greenhouse. There might be something back there that needs digging up."

"Have you gone mad? You can't do that."

"Mr. Chilton, I'm going to need you to take a trip down to the station while we get this sorted out."

"I will do no such thing."

The sheriff turned to his deputies. "You boys take Mr. Chilton down to the station house and introduce him to our deluxe accommodations."

"I am a close personal friend of the governor."

"We'll be sure to tell him you said 'hello' if we happen to bump in to him," one of the deputies said as he took hold of Chilton's arm and escorted him away.

The entire crowd was in a state of shock. Nobody was more shocked than me. I hadn't seen that one coming. What began as a calculated bluff had exploded beyond anything I had ever imagined.

I looked over Katherine's way. She was standing three bodies down from Bradley. Both their jaws were hanging open and Bradley looked like someone had just run over his puppy. It looked like the shock of seeing his father carted away had taken a lot out of him.

As I approached Katherine, I could see the nervousness take hold of her body. Her eyes were fixed on mine, wide and scared.

"In my breast pocket there's a pack of smokes."

She fished in my jacket and pulled out the cigarettes and

lighter. With shaky fingers, she placed one in my mouth and lit it for me. "What's next? Are you going to pull a rabbit from your hat?"

I took in a long drag and let it out, the cigarette dangling from my lips. "No, something bigger."

Chilton had been handcuffed and taken away by one of the deputies. Another deputy escorted a distraught and confused Harriet Chilton away. There was a lot of talk going on around me, the crowd whispering amongst themselves, disbelief lingering in the air. The sheriff's voice boomed over the crowd noise.

"Ok, McKeller, maybe you just solved a twenty-year-old murder case and maybe you didn't. That still leaves us with the Tucker Morgan matter. Do you want to explain how an envelope with fifteen hundred dollars ended up in your room?"

I was still staring into Katherine's eyes. Bright, dark and piercing, the nervousness gone from them, replaced with the confidence I was used to seeing. I wondered if she knew something I didn't or if she was just underestimating the hold her gaze had on me.

"Chilton paid me to look into the Morgan murder. It wasn't fifteen bills but it was a nice wad of cash. He wanted me to keep him apprised as to how the investigation was going. I got the feeling he wasn't so much interested in who killed Tucker as he was how he and his were implicated." I replied with the cigarette in my mouth.

"So where did the extra loot come from?"

"I'm guessing Chet Bowman planted it there last night after he worked me over." I hadn't looked up from Katherine's eyes.

"So, who killed Tucker Morgan?"

I motioned for Katherine to take the cigarette from my mouth. She did, turning it around and placing it in hers, taking a long slow drag. I didn't even know she smoked.

Our eyes were locked, as though we were the only two people there, as if no one else mattered. I could imagine the tiny wheels behind them working away, wondering what my next move would be, how many skeletons I was willing to uncover. She looked certain that she had me where she wanted me, like she knew her secrets were safe with me.

"So, how long did he tell you you'd have to wait, a year, two years?"

Katherine squinted and smiled, like she didn't understand the question.

"How long were you supposed to wait for Bradley to divorce Lucy?"

"Divorce Lucy? That's awfully pessimistic, they haven't even married yet."

"That was the plan, wasn't it?"

"I don't know what you're talking about."

I turned to the right and took two steps so I was standing smack dab in front of my best friend, or at least the guy I had thought of as my best friend the day before. My mind was racing and there were conflicting thoughts battling it out in my head. Maybe I did owe him and maybe I didn't.

Earlier in the day I had been ready to walk away and let it lie but now things had been turned around, topsy-turvy. Somebody's throat was going into a noose and I sure didn't want it to be mine.

"I'm curious, Bradley, was this all about greed or did this all come about because of how much you hate your father?"

"Frankie, what are you talking about?"

"It's obvious you hated the man. Why wouldn't you? He ruled your life with an iron fist. You couldn't make a move without his permission. He belittled you and undermined you every chance he got. When you went to him with your plan to turn Myrtle Beach into a vacation paradise he laughed in your face. He told you how stupid your plan was, that the future of this town was in industry and agriculture."

"It wasn't like that at all."

"There was also the little matter of turning your mother into a zombie. How bad did that get under your skin? It must have been tough to see someone you love wither away into a shell of her former self, knowing all along that he was the one responsible."

Bradley looked around nervously, trying to force a smile on his face but it only stuck a couple of seconds. He was jittery and uneasy, nothing like the Bradley I had always known.

"You would have done anything to get back at him. What

you really wanted was to go out on your own and show him what you could do, rub it in his face. The problem with that was Daddy controlled the purse strings. Without his money you were lost. You needed backing. You needed land.

"Your girlfriend's family had land and she was more than happy to give you control of it. Hell, it probably sounded like just the thing to fix her financial woes. The problem was her land was almost worthless. Even when you found out about the highway they were planning, it sat too far off. There was no access."

Bradley was fidgeting more than ever, a light sweat breaking out on his forehead. Truth be told, I was flying on a wing and a prayer and it wasn't until I saw his reaction that I realized I was on the right path.

"Now, Lucy's family, they had land too. Their land sat between Katherine's and the highway. It was the plot you needed to make your plan work. Without the Fleming land your dream of a world class golf and beach resort would die a quick painful death.

"I imagine it was Gilbert you first took the proposal to. My guess is he loved the idea. It was just the kind of get rich quick scheme that Gilbert lived for. The thing is Gilbert didn't wield a lot of power where his family's holdings were concerned. Being the recluse he was, his father wasn't about to turn over the family business to him.

"After what happened between Herbert Fleming and your father, he wasn't about to turn it over to you either. He'd learned his lesson about dealing with the Chiltons. With dealing with anyone outside of the family, for that matter.

"That's when you realized the way to get control of the Fleming land was to become part of the family. That's when you decided to marry Lucy."

He started to say something but nothing came out.

"It was a pretty good plan really. Everybody wins. You marry Lucy and build your resort. You get rich, Katherine gets rich, even the Flemings get rich and the best part is you did it all without the help of your father. Can you imagine how infuriated the old geezer would be when he found out?

"Here's where things get messy. Tucker Morgan found out about what was going on. Dorothy was supposed to keep her mouth shut about the highway but her and Tuck were friends. She felt guilty and she went to him with what she knew, which wasn't much. That was a few days ago. It probably took him that long to figure out what was going on, but Tucker was a pretty bright guy and he figured it out.

"That was what the fight between him and Gilbert was about. He was going to your father. He tried to tell him that first night in the hotel but, being the stubborn bastard that he is, your father blew him off. It was only a matter of time before he had your father's ear. Once that happened, your plans were ruined."

"No."

"Gilbert was pretty angry but not to the point of murder. He'd had enough deals fall through that he wasn't going to let it get to him too much. Gilbert dealt with the news in his usual fashion. He took his lady friend to a gin mill and proceeded to tie one on.

"You, on the other hand, couldn't let it go. This was your big opportunity. This was the chance of a lifetime and if it passed you by you knew you might never get another. Without this deal you would end up at your father's mercy for the rest of your life. You couldn't let that happen."

"I didn't kill Tucker Morgan."

"Maybe you didn't mean to. Maybe you went there to reason with him, bribe him. Maybe you went to scare him, I don't know. Things got out of hand."

"No, it's not like that."

"However it happened, Tucker Morgan ended up dead. You told the police you were one of the first ones on the scene, you weren't. You came from a lot farther than two doors away."

"No."

"That's ridiculous," Lucy said, protecting her fiancé until the end.

"You tried to bribe me because you knew I was getting close."

"No."

"You reached out and shut the door because you knew your prints were already on the handle."

"No."

I turned to the Sheriff. "I assume you have dusted for prints?"

"Of course we have. There were at least three sets on the outside of the door, maybe two on the inside. We've just begun going through the hotel employees, matching them up. We were planning on beginning to gather prints from the guests this afternoon, until — "

"Until you found your suspect in me."

Sheriff Talbert shrugged. "There didn't seem to be any need to inconvenience everyone if we had our man."

"I believe you'll find Bradley's prints all over that room."

"No, you wouldn't," Bradley pleaded.

"Bradley only pulled the door shut," Lucy added, still protective of him.

"There's one way to find out," I suggested to the sheriff. "Dust the room."

"I'm telling you, I didn't kill anyone."

"Of course you did, Bradley. You were the only one with enough motive and means to do it."

"No. It's not like that." Bradley looked disoriented and shaken. He was sweating profusely and pale. "Ok, you're right about the deal. Everything you said about the land and Katherine and marrying Lucy but I didn't kill Tucker, I swear."

"You did it, Bradley. There are only two reasons people ever murder, greed and love, you did it for greed."

"He didn't do it," Katherine spoke up, turning all of our attentions to her. "He didn't kill Tucker."

"Well, I would expect you to think so. You're in love with him, after all."

"No, you don't understand. I know he didn't kill Tucker. He was with me. We were on the beach, out by the dunes, when we heard the shot."

Sheriff Talbert asked Bradley if it were true. He nodded.

"After I walked Lucy to her room I went out to the beach and met Katherine. We were there when the shot went off."

"They're lying," I said.

"No … we're not," Katherine answered with a soft sincere tone in her voice and a look in her eye that told me she wasn't.

There were more murmurings and mutterings from the crowd.

I was dumbstruck. It wouldn't have taken more than a feather to knock me over. I had been on such a roll, how could I have been so off? Everything that had seemed so clear moments before exploded in my head and I was left with a jumble of half facts, guesstimations and observations that no longer made sense. It was like a calculus problem I couldn't wrap my brain around. Like I said earlier, I'm really not very good at this detective stuff.

"I think we've played this game long enough," Sheriff Talbert said as his men took hold of my arms again and began to pull me toward the door.

Panic swept over me and I scanned the faces in the crowd looking for an answer. Bradley was still pale and shaken, Katherine looked concerned and sad. Gilbert, smug and satisfied, maybe more than a little relieved. Lucy, prim and perfect …

"Stop!"

For some reason the deputies paused for a moment, awaiting further orders from the sheriff. It was time for my last ditch effort.

I looked hard into the eyes of Lucy Fleming. "How did you know?"

Confusion ruled her face and she glanced around nervous like. "How did I know what?"

"How did you know Bradley only pulled the door shut? How did you know he didn't touch anything else?"

She paused. "I don't know. I guess he told me."

"It's not really the kind of thing that comes up in casual conversation, especially if he did it without thinking. Did you tell her, Bradley?"

Bradley didn't answer. He was shooting a weird look toward his fiancé.

"You knew because you were there, Lucy. Where were you, on the balcony, behind the curtain?"

Lucy gave a half laugh. "Don't be silly."

"You were still there when we came in. You didn't have time to get away. When Bradley closed the door, you made your escape over the balcony on to the next, working your way down the length of the hotel. You were a gymnast, after all. It would have been easy for you. That's why you were the last to get there."

"I thought you had come running from your room, that's why you were so out of breath, but you had gone back to your room to change clothes. You also came from the other direction. Everyone else came from the north where the elevator is but you came from the south end of the building. You had worked your way down the balconies and came back up the stairs. That's what took you so long after the gunshot, why you were the last to arrive. That's how you twisted your ankle, why you didn't want to play tennis with Katherine."

"That's absurd."

It was all beginning to come together in my head. "Of course, you had just as much to lose as Bradley did, maybe more. Without the land deal you stood to lose the man you loved."

"You think I killed Tucker?"

"Why not? He was the one thing standing between you and happiness. You said yourself that you had been in love with Bradley forever, all those years fawning over him, dreaming of being together, watching him with Katherine. How bad did that eat at you? How hard was it to see the man you loved with another woman?"

"No ... "

"You would have done anything to be with Bradley. You said it yourself."

"No ... "

"I'm guessing the fact that Tucker royally screwed your family over years before didn't make it any harder to pull the trigger."

She closed her eyes and began shaking her head from side to side, refusing to hear my accusations.

"You probably found out about the deal from Gilbert. A couple of drinks in him and he's bound to spill the beans on anything he's got in the works, especially if it makes him look like a big shot. From what I gather, he loves to run his mouth when he's half in the bag."

"Hey—" Gilbert started but I cut him off.

"That gun I asked you about, where is it?"

Gilbert gave me one of those 'I don't know what you're talking about' looks.

"Enough with the games, Gilbert, tell me about the gun, unless you want to end up with an accessory to murder rap hanging around your neck. The gun, where is it?"

Gilbert looked suddenly small and weak. "I don't know."

"But you had it with you on this trip, didn't you? You always had it nearby. Not because you needed it for anything in particular but because it made you feel like a big man."

"You had a gun go missing and you failed to mention it?" Sheriff Talbert asked.

"Everyone already suspected me of killing Tucker. What was I supposed to say? Oh by the way, somebody stole my pistol?"

The sheriff stepped in toward me and whipped me around so he was right in my face. His was red and angry, his eyes wide with anger. "What are you trying to pull here? You knew about the missing gun, maybe you stole it. Maybe your plan is to go through and accuse everyone at the wedding in hopes of confusing us country bumpkins into thinking you're innocent."

"There's one way to find out."

"How's that?"

"Dust the room for Lucy's prints."

"All of the prints on the door were too large to be Lucy's. They most likely belong to men."

"Her prints wouldn't be on the door," I explained. "She would have knocked and Tucker would have let her in. He would have shut the door behind her, gentleman that he was.

"Look for Lucy's prints out back, the balcony door, the railing, the balcony next door. That's where you'll find her prints and there's only one reason they'd be there."

From off to my right I heard the shuffle of satin and lace, a white blur making a move in my peripheral. I looked up just in time to see Lucy lunge forward, slamming into the back of Sheriff Talbert, pulling his revolver from his holster as she did.

Little pretty Lucy stood there in white, two hands holding the gun in front of her, aiming it at me. Something old, something new, something borrowed, something burnish blue to kill people with.

Tears were rolling down her face, her eyes red and swollen. Her small hands were having difficulty holding the weapon steady through her sobs.

"You ruined everything," she said.

"Lucy," Bradley tried.

"No! Stay back. I'll shoot, I swear I will."

"You better listen to her, Bradley. She's done it before."

"You think I didn't know why you were marrying me?" She had turned the gun away from me and had it set on Bradley. "You think I didn't know about you and Katherine? I just thought that once we were married things would be different. I knew that you would learn to love me in time.

"I've always loved you, Bradley. I just wanted us to be together. I was willing to look past everything for the chance to make it work. Once we were married Katherine would be out of the picture. Later there would be children and a life together and I knew I could make you happy if you would just give me the chance."

"Lucy, no … "

"Once we were married, I knew everything would be all right. I knew that I could make it work if I only had the chance. I loved you, Bradley. I would have done anything for you."

"Even murder," I added.

"Tucker was going to spoil everything. He was going to go to Mr. Chilton with everything he knew. Once it was out in the open I knew you wouldn't marry me. I knew without my family's land you wouldn't want me. I couldn't let that happen."

"You knew about Gilbert's gun?" I asked. She didn't answer. "Sure you did. I'll wager Gilbert wasn't lying when he told us the two of you walked to his room. You had to go to his room. You needed his gun. While he was primping for his big date you swiped it from the room. Then you came back to the party and let Bradley walk you to your room, the perfect alibi. After he went down to meet Katherine you headed to Tucker's room."

Lucy didn't respond.

"Where's the gun now?"

Lucy Paused. "I threw it in the ocean."

"Lucy, this can't be true," Katherine said in a sympathetic tone.

"You shut up, you filthy whore. If it weren't for you none of this would have happened, if you would have just gone away." She looked back to Bradley. "You know she slept with your best friend, don't you? She told me so. I was going to tell you all about it after we were married. She's a slut, Bradley. She's not good enough for you."

I didn't have the heart to tell her he already knew about Katherine and me, that it had been part of their plan all along.

Bradley was staring back at his would be bride with a look somewhere between sadness and terror in his eyes, like he was looking at a complete stranger.

"It's not too late. We could go away. We could disappear. We could still be together." Lucy seemed to believe her words.

"We can't. This has gone too far. I never meant to hurt anybody, especially not you. I thought I had it all worked out. I was going to make us all rich."

"We don't need to be rich, Bradley. We just need to be together. That's all we ever needed. Why couldn't you see that?"

"I'm sorry, Lucy."

"You should have loved me, Bradley."

The tears were still streaming down her cheeks but her face seemed to take on a clarity, like she'd reached an inspired decision. I figured that wasn't such a good sign.

With her thumb, she cocked back the hammer of the revolver, holding it pointed toward Bradley. "I love you, Bradley," she sighed.

It was now or never. I lowered my shoulder and charged into her. Knocking her arm off to the side as the gun went off. We went flying across a china breakfast setting, toppling a table as I took her down. With no arms to break my fall, I landed face first on the concrete floor, Lucy wedged under my torso, kicking and clawing.

"Get off me! Let me up!" She was digging into my face with her nails, ranting and raving about how much she hated me, how I had ruined everything. It seemed like an eternity before they finally lifted me up by the arms and pulled her away from me.

She'd gotten me a good one in the left eye and I watched through blood and stinging pain as they restrained and cuffed

211

the pretty brunette. She looked more like an animal than the reserved and petite girl I had met a few days before. Little pretty Lucy was dragged off hissing and snarling while the collection of wedding guests watched in shock and horror.

Eventually they got around to un-cuffing me, as it didn't seem to be a big priority for the sheriff and his deputies during the commotion. By that time my arms were numb and the pain in my shoulder blades was excruciating. Many of the guests had wandered off after Lucy was taken away and only a few of us were left behind. Sheriff Talbert was the first to approach me. He handed me an envelope.

"I think this belongs to you."

"Isn't that some sort of evidence?"

"We found it in your room. Now that you've been cleared of all charges I don't see where it concerns us how you got it."

"Thanks."

"Off the record, I still don't like private dicks."

"Shucks, Sheriff, and here I thought you were going to ask me to the spring dance."

"I can't help but think if you would have come forward with some of this information a lot of this could have been avoided."

"I'll keep that in mind next time."

"Let's make sure there is no next time."

I stuffed the envelope into my pocket as the good sheriff took his leave. Bradley and Katherine were next. They both stood in front of me, none of us knowing what to say.

"Look," I started, "that stuff I said — "

"Forget it. You were pretty dead on with a lot of it." He seemed embarrassed and awkward. He barely resembled the good friend I loved the day before. "I guess you saved my ass this time."

"In a round about way … "

"Even?"

"Even."

He smiled at me but it was a distant smile, not the kind of smile you get from a friend. I guess there is such thing as too much water under the bridge. I knew in that moment Bradley and I would never be close again. Everything has its price.

He walked off without another word. Katherine stayed back for a moment. She looked lost and searching for the right words.

"I'm really sorry about everything," she finally said.

"So am I."

"What you must think of me." If she only knew.

"Everybody has their skeletons."

Her perfect face was pink with embarrassment and she looked smaller than I remembered, maybe a little less lady like. She smiled, but hers was nothing like Bradley's. Maybe it was but I wanted it to be more. What can I say? I'm a sucker for a pretty face.

Katherine leaned over and gave me a light kiss on the cheek before turning and running after Bradley. Long after the cuts and bruises would heal on my face and the pain was long gone I would still be able to feel her kiss on my cheek.

Chapter Twenty-Nine

*T*he next day I let myself sleep in, a little treat to myself. The swelling in my face had gone down a bit but the pain was worse. By the time I got up, packed and ready, it was late afternoon and I climbed into the elevator with my suitcase. Guess who was working?

"Good morning, sir," Freckle Face said with a grin.

I nodded.

"So, are you checking out today?"

I looked down at the suitcase in my hand and back up to the kid. "No, I just thought I'd take my luggage for a walk."

Freckle Face laughed an uncomfortable laugh. "Good one."

We reached the main floor and the doors opened. I started to get out but stopped and turned back to the kid. I reached into my coat pocket and he stiffened. Who knows what he thought I was going for.

I took out a twenty spot and was handing it to him when I noticed, for the first time, he was wearing a name tag. Who knew Freckle Face even had a name? "Thanks for the rides, Clifford."

"Thank you, sir."

"No problem. One more thing … "

"Yes sir?"

"Clifford, get out of this shoe box every once in awhile. Go out and see the sunshine, breathe some fresh air."

"Yes sir."

I decided he wasn't such a bad kid.

From there I went to the main desk to check out and pay my bill. The desk clerk didn't seem too interested in taking my money but instead asked me to wait while he got the manager. I tried to think if I had broken anything, if maybe Chet Bowman busted up some furniture while he was busting up me.

The manager was a tall stocky man with squared features and a strange beard that grew out from under his chin and tucked around his lower face. It reminded me of gills and he looked kind of like a fish in a three piece suit. His name was Buntemeyer.

I had seen him around the hotel over the past few days but I hadn't had the opportunity to meet him. It was just the same, as far as I was concerned, as he looked like the intense and serious type, hardly the kind I was likely to pal around with.

"I just wanted to tell you how grateful we are for everything you did," Buntemeyer said to me, trying to avoid staring at my swollen face.

"Don't mention it."

"It's just that an unsolved murder can be very bad for business and all."

"I can imagine."

"Everyone's talking about the splendid job you did, solving two murders. You've brought quite a bit of notoriety to our hotel."

"Yeah, well, I got lucky is all."

"I can't thank you enough, in fact ... "

I shrugged, still wondering where he was going with the conversation.

"Well, it's just that, not only would we like to comp your stay, but if you'd like to stick around for a few more days we'd be happy to take care of it."

"You're telling me that I can stay for free in the Ocean Forest Hotel?"

"Yes. If you decide to take us up on our offer I have a little something I'd like to discuss with you."

"What would that be?"

"It's just that we were considering hiring a full time house detective and I thought you might … "

"You're offering me a job?" It was about the last thing I had expected to hear. A house dick sounded like a pretty sweet gig. Basically, it would entail becoming sort of a head security guy and many of the larger hotels in the country employed them.

Buntemeyer shrugged and nodded. "I know you have a thriving business up north but if you'd consider taking us up on our offer I think we could make it worth your while. And of course you would have your own room in the hotel."

"I would live in the Ocean Forest Hotel?"

"Yes. Most of our employees stay at the bullpen across the street but we'd want you to stay on the premises."

I looked around, soaking in the grandeur and luxury surrounding me. A few days ago I didn't know people lived like this. Now I had an offer to set up house in one of the finest hotels on the east coast.

I couldn't help but wonder how long it would take Buntemeyer to figure out I had no idea what I was doing where detecting was concerned, that I was basically a hack faking my way through.

"Can I think about it for a few days?"

"Of course, take your time."

That was that. I had my bag sent back up to the room and I asked the desk clerk to call me a cab.

"Where are you heading?"

"Atlantic Beach."

The clerk looked at me like I was crazy. I guess they didn't get a lot of guests heading that way. Not guests with my pigmentation, anyway. What did I care? I needed to see a friendly face and I couldn't think of one friendlier than Tabby's, the girl I met at Mack's Dive. A shot of hooch didn't sound bad either.

Chapter Thirty

Lucy Fleming was sentenced to life in prison for the murder of Tucker Morgan. She had tried the insanity angle but the jury didn't buy it. If not for her youthful good looks she might have ended up in the chair. Jury's don't typically like sending pretty girls to their death, they're funny that way.

Old man Chilton didn't get off as lightly. After the Charleston police found the body of Michael Tate buried on the estate grounds, he was convicted of murder in the first degree. The old buzzard spent a fortune on his defense. He was electrocuted less than a year later.

Chet Bowman was charged with accessory to murder. He was sentenced to five years but with good behavior he could be out in three. I'm guessing he'll serve the entire five.

Sheriff Talbert offered to charge him with assault as well, if I agreed to press charges. I didn't see the point. As far as I was concerned, Bowman and I were pretty close to square.

Talbert got a lot of press after the arrests of two murderers in one day. It was about two more than Myrtle Beach sees in an average year. He still serves as sheriff, running the town like he owns it. There's talk of him making a run at mayor, but I don't see it happening. I can't picture the good sheriff in a three piece suit, hobnobbing with politicians, playing golf with the governor. My guess is he's pretty happy where he is, as happy as Sheriff Talbert gets, at least.

Gilbert Fleming still pokes his head in and out of the area from time to time. When he does it's usually to do with some big deal he has in the works. To my knowledge, he's still waiting for one to come through for him. You have to admire his perseverance.

Herbert and Lydia Fleming still live in Charleston. They rarely make it to the beach anymore after the scandal with their daughter. Word is Herbert sold all his holdings in Myrtle Beach and invested in a string of economy motels. They're not exactly the Ocean Forest but they're very popular with families and business travelers. I guess he's doing OK for himself.

Harriet Chilton managed to keep the family estate in Charleston. They say she spends her days there, lounging out behind the greenhouse, sipping tea.

Bradley inherited the family business. He invested everything he had in a luxurious golf and beach resort. Unfortunately, the highway he was banking on never came through, not in time to save his investment anyway. He lost pretty much everything. The last I heard, he was working for a real estate firm in Columbia, South Carolina. They say the old man who runs it is a real son of a bitch.

He and Katherine didn't survive his financial ruin.

Seven months after the ordeal, Katherine gave birth to a baby boy, Franklin Bradford Mathews. Rumors swarmed around about whether the baby's father was Bradley Chilton or some gumshoe from up north. Katherine never said one way or the other. I guess she figured it was nobody's business.

Every month I send her a check. It's not much and I'm not even sure why I do it, but with all the financial bad luck she's had I'm sure she can use it. She ended up selling off most everything her family had left and bought a small house in downtown Charleston. That's what I hear, anyway. She's never actually contacted me, not even acknowledging my monthly payments. She does, however, always cash the checks.

I took the offer to stay on at the Ocean Forest. There was nothing waiting for me back in Baltimore. Besides, Myrtle Beach was starting to grow on me.

She was small and unrefined but there was something about her, like a budding flower on the verge of blooming. It was still anybody's guess how she'd turn out but she had potential in the way young girls do when they approach maturity, when you're still uncertain if they're going to end up becoming dames or ladies. I figured I might as well stick around and find out for myself. Maybe I could even play a minor role in her outcome in some small insignificant way.

There was also the Atlantic. We still had our differences and it wasn't likely we'd ever be friends but I could never deny the link we shared.

She had played a major part in what I was and who I was. I had left a part of myself in her that day on Omaha Beach. She owned something that belonged to me. Maybe by living here beside her I could one day find a way to take it back. Then again, maybe I was just fooling myself.

The End

www.theoceanforest.com

Coming in 2012 from
INGALLS PUBLISHING GROUP

Damn Yankee
MURDER IN MYRTLE BEACH
by Troy D. Nooe

ANOTHER FRANKIE MCKELLER MYSTERY

MORE GREAT MYSTERIES FROM

Ingalls Publishing Group, Inc

The Ninth Man
by Brad Crowther

2010 winner of the Black Orchid Novella Award sponsored by
Alfred Hitchcock's Mystery Magazine and The Wolfe Pack

The Ninth Man, a modern-day mystery set in Charleston, South Carolina, revolves around a fictional diary kept by a Union spy that explains the disappearance of the H.L. Hunley, a Confederate fishboat that became the world's first successful combat submarine when it sank a Union ship blockading Charleston Harbor.

ISBN: 978-1-932158-92-2, November 1, 2011

One Shot Too Many
AN APPALACHIAN ADVENTURE MYSTERY
by Maggie Bishop

Yesterday's regret; today's deadly fix. Impulsive acts from the past return to haunt, resulting in the death of a popular photo-journalist near the cozy mountain town of Boone, NC. Detective Tucker must face his own past while investigating suspects determined to keep too many secrets. Did the victim take too many photos of one of them? Jemma Chase, trail-ride leader and CSI wannabe, follows clues, even though her interference may cost Tucker his job.

Fifth in the series of stand-alone APPALACHIAN ADVENTURES

ISBN: 978-1-932158-95-3, October 1, 2011

Nationally available in bookstores,
from Amazon and other and online retailers
www.ingallspublishinggroup.com

CPSIA information can be obtained at www.ICGtesting.com
Printed in the USA
LVOW061926150911

246433LV00002B/4/P

9 781932 158915